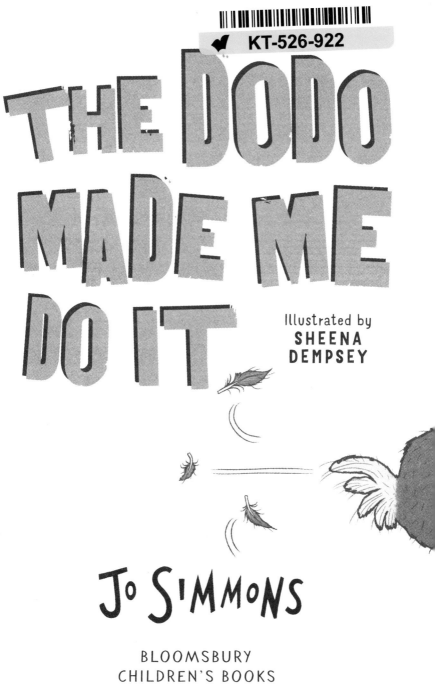

THE DODO MADE ME DO IT

Illustrated by
SHEENA DEMPSEY

JO SIMMONS

BLOOMSBURY
CHILDREN'S BOOKS
LONDON OXFORD NEW YORK NEW DELHI SYDNEY

DU

The
rea

THE DODO MADE ME DO IT

BLOOMSBURY CHILDREN'S BOOKS
Bloomsbury Publishing Plc
50 Bedford Square, London, WC1B 3DP, UK

BLOOMSBURY, BLOOMSBURY CHILDREN'S BOOKS and the Diana logo
are trademarks of Bloomsbury Publishing Plc

First published in Great Britain in 2018 by Bloomsbury Publishing Plc

Text copyright © Jo Simmons, 2018
Illustrations copyright © Sheena Dempsey, 2018

Jo Simmons has asserted her right under the Copyright, Designs
and Patents Act, 1988, to be identified as Author of this work

A catalogue record for this book is available from the British Library

ISBN: PB: 978-1-4088-7777-7; eBook: 978-1-4088-7778-4

2 4 6 8 10 9 7 5 3 1

Typeset by RefineCatch Limited, Bungay, Suffolk
Printed and bound in Great Britain by CPI Group (UK) Ltd, Croydon CR0 4YY

To find ou nsbury.com

Chapter 1

SCOTLAND

WELCOME TO
SCOTLAND

'Woo-hoo!' yelled Danny's mum, as they drove past the huge blue sign by the motorway. 'Only another four hours and we'll be at Granny's!'

Danny, sitting in the back of the car, narrowed his big blue eyes and stared at the dull, rolling scenery as it sped by. There was no 'woo-hoo' from him. Not even a quiet 'yay'! He wasn't happy. It was the start of the summer holidays and he had to spend all six weeks of it with his Granny Flora. This was a problem for four key reasons:

1. Granny Flora did crosswords all the time and was obsessed with porridge
2. It rained a lot in Kinoussie
3. There was nothing to do and nothing ever happened, *ever*
4. The people in Kinoussie were all weird

'Come on, love,' said Danny's mum. 'I know you don't want to go, but Dad and I have to work again this summer. Dad is off at sea, and Old Hodge Podge says I can't have the time off.'

Danny's dad wasn't a sailor. He was a trumpet player in a band on a cruise ship that puttered around the Mediterranean. Summer was his busiest time.

Danny's mum didn't work for Old Hodge Podge either. At least, that wasn't his name. He was really called Ken Hodgson of Hodgson's Hanging Baskets. Mum worked as a gardener for him. Summer was her busiest time too.

So, for as long as Danny could remember, he went to Kinoussie in the summer, to stay with Granny Flora. Holiday guides called Kinoussie 'A quaint and remote jewel, untouched by time, on Scotland's stunning west coast'. To Danny, it was a total fun-desert, populated by weirdies and oldies and oldie wierdies. With midges.

'Untouched by time' was about right though. Granny didn't even have Wi-Fi.

'Perhaps you could meet up with Susie?' said Danny's mum.

Danny groaned and slapped his forehead.

'You say that every year!' he protested. 'Just because Susie is the only other ten-year-old living within three billion miles of Granny's house doesn't mean we're friends!'

Danny hardly knew Susie. He'd met her once last year. While his mum and her mum and Granny Flora had tea, Susie had sat in the corner, buried in a science book. She barely spoke to him.

'I know she's a bit science-mad and bookish,' said Danny's mum, 'but she'd be someone to run around with, unlike Granny, who prefers to …'

'Do the crossword!' exploded Danny. 'And when she's not doing the crossword she's driving Mrs McWhatsername to her hospital appointments or taking someone's chicken to the vet.'

'She's a pillar of the community!' Danny's mum laughed. 'Always ready to help her neighbours. They all look after each other in the village. They share everything. No secrets in Kinoussie!'

Danny went back to staring out of the

window. A depressed-looking horse stood motionless in a wet field. He knew how it felt. He reached for his backpack and pulled out a copy of his favourite comic – *Zac Hanaway, Space Runaway.* Zac was a boy who had escaped from his prison planet and now raced around the galaxy, having adventures with his two trusty companions, Chips the Robot and a beautiful talking hawk called Zena. Danny wanted to have adventures like Zac. He wanted to *be* Zac: cool, brave and free to journey through space and time, seeking out adventures and new lands. Not Scotland though. He'd give that a miss.

'I bet Zac Hanaway's never been to Kinoussie,' muttered Danny as he flicked through the comic. 'He'd last about five minutes, then leave because it's so boring!'

'Next year!' said Danny's mum, glancing at him in the mirror again. 'I *absolutely* promise that next year we will go some-where different. Look, I grew up here and I loved it, and Granny grew up here and loved it too. In fact, she never left. Lived here all her life.'

Danny said nothing. The thought of living in Kinoussie all your life left him speechless.

'It is beautiful, isn't it? There's tons of space, and the beach at Clootie Bay is so close, and there's wildlife …'

'Midges,' muttered Danny.

'Anyway,' his mum added, 'I've packed the cool box with taramasalata this year, since Granny can't get it in the Spar.'

Danny looked at the cool box by his feet and imagined the pots of pink, fishy spread in there. Yum. At least he had that. How he loved taramasalata. Great with crackers. Or pitta.

'You can make this work, Danny!' said his mum. 'There is fun to be had up here. You just have to make it happen!'

Chapter 2

ADVENTURE?

Tap, tap, tap, tap. Gunfire. Bullets. No! Spears. Tiny ice javelins, hurled by deadly assassin snow hamsters, wearing charm-woven armour. Use your shield, Danny! Quick, use your …!

'Waarrgghh!' Danny sat up in bed, blinking. Just a dream. There were no assassin snow hamsters. It was just the Scottish rain beating against his bedroom window. He pulled back the curtains, made from cream fabric with tiny roses, chosen a lifetime ago by his mum when this was her room. Outside, her car was gone. She was already driving home.

Granny Flora's farmhouse was squat and square, and Danny's room was on the side, its window looking down over the single-storey outbuilding that was built alongside. Beyond, there was the old stone barn, standing empty as usual, and Danny could just make out Granny's friend Roddy Aye feeding the chickens in a fenced coop further off, oblivious to the summer downpour.

'Rain and Roddy and nothing else,' Danny muttered. 'Typical.'

Danny thought of his best friend, Cal, who always went on great holidays. Last year, he went to Australia for three weeks. At Easter, he did a city break in Paris. This summer, he was in the USA. What was he up to now? Eating a giant hamburger? Tracking grizzly bears in the mountains? Riding a moose and wearing full cowboy outfit? Did they have moose (or mooses or meece) in the USA? Who knew. All Danny knew was that he was in Kinoussie again. Excitement factor: zero. Possibility of excitement occurring: also zero.

As Danny dressed, he made the same wish he always made when he arrived at his granny's house for the summer: that something exciting might happen. But what? What was even possible here in Kinoussie? A helicopter piloted by kittens landing in the farmyard? A crack appearing in the fabric of time, just to the left of Granny's chicken coop? Roddy Aye saying no for once (all Roddy ever said was 'aye')?

'Has anything exciting ever happened here?' Danny asked his granny when he got downstairs. She was sitting at the kitchen table, working on a crossword, several pencils stuck into her messy bun of thick grey hair. The muggy, oaty scent of porridge filled the air.

'Exciting?' she asked, like she hadn't tried the word out for some decades.

'Yes, you know – an adventure, fun, something a bit woo!' said Danny.

Granny Flora put her crossword down and stuck her pencil in her hair, creating an Aztec-style headdress of HBs.

'Roddy, has anything exciting happened here?' she shouted over her shoulder.

Danny hadn't spotted Roddy, sitting in the chimney nook by the fire, knitting quietly.

'Aye!' he said, in an 'of course' kind of way.

'Ah yes!' said Granny. 'There was that time old Murdo McMurdo was snowed in for six days and lived on cat food and turnips. About ten years ago, wasn't it, Roddy?'

'Aye,' said Roddy, nodding.

Danny frowned and fidgeted, tucking his long legs under him on the chair.

'What about a proper exciting event, that actually happened, you know, not just getting snowed in or a goat escaping or someone buying the wrong kind of jam by mistake,' Danny said. 'What about when you were a child? Did you get up to mischief or have adventures?'

'Let me see,' said Granny Flora.

She thought for ages. Danny was about to give up when she grabbed a pencil from her hair and held it upright like an exclamation mark.

'Ha!' she said. 'The lighthouse! That's right! I'd forgotten, but now I remember. One night my brother Jamie broke into the old lighthouse just away down the coast from here.'

'And?' asked Danny.

'We lit it!' said Granny Flora, her blue eyes twinkling.

'You were there too?'

'I brought the matches!' she said. 'It was just an oil lamp, easy enough to light. The beam stretched for miles. Quite beautiful really. Do you remember, Roddy?'

'Aye,' said Roddy, nodding eagerly.

'That was the first and only time I ever saw that lighthouse lit. It was closed just before I was born. No need for it now, but there had been a shipwreck on the tiny island in Clootie Bay. That's why they put it there in the first place.'

Danny spluttered and sprayed a mouthful of milk across the tablecloth.

'A what what? Did I hear you right, Granny? A *shipwreck*? Here? In Kinoussie? Tell me more!'

'There's not much to tell,' said Granny Flora. 'It was a Dutch ship, I believe, blown off course by a huge storm and then dashed on the rocks! No survivors. It was a very long time ago. Now, how about some porridge?'

By the time Danny had forced down a small bowl of porridge it had stopped raining. By the time he had finished brushing his teeth, he had made a plan. A plan for A&E: Adventure & Excitement! The A&E plan went like this:

1. Go down to Clootie Bay and get on to the island. (Not sure how, detail to follow)
2. Discover ancient treasure scattered there from the shipwreck
3. Sell it and make lots of ££s
4. Buy a train ticket home and surprise Mum
5. Then book a really fab holiday with all the money. Somewhere hot, where they don't eat porridge. Somewhere even better than where Cal goes, so he's jealous

It was a brilliant, simple plan spoiled only by the sound of a knock on the door and a girl's voice calling out hello. Danny peeped downstairs.

Susie! The science-nut, book-mad girl from the village was chatting to Granny Flora in the hall. She had grown a bit since he first met her last summer. Her dead-straight hair was cut in a cool bob now, with a super-sharp fringe, and she was wearing a pair of round glasses.

'Susie's here!' said Granny Flora.

Susie's small, intense eyes followed Danny as he ran downstairs.

'I was just going out,' he told her. 'Coming?'

Danny ran across Granny's big front yard, splashing through puddles, and on to the path to Clootie Bay. Despite carrying a back-pack filled with books and magazines, Susie soon caught up with him, and the children slowed to a walking pace.

'My mum told me to come and say hello …' Susie said. 'She thinks it will be good for me to hang out with someone.'

'Aren't there other children near here?'

Danny asked. 'Friends?'

'Have you seen the people in Kinoussie, Danny?' Susie laughed. 'Not young! So why are you up here again, then?'

'My mum has to work all summer, and my dad, so ...'

'My mum works all the time too,' said Susie. 'During the week she's the ticket inspector on the Fort Plother to Isle of Bladda ferry, on Saturdays she covers for Donald in the Spar, while he does his part-time sheep maintenance course, and in the summer on Sundays she mows the grass at Scotland's smallest campsite, in the village.'

'I don't want to do lots of jobs like Mum though, when I grow up,' Susie went on. 'I want to be a scientist. Perhaps a zoologist, or maybe a palaeoecologist.'

'A palaeo-say-what-now?' asked Danny.

'It's someone who examines interactions

between different organisms or between different organisms and the environment,' she said, eyes sparkling. 'What do you want to do when you grow up?'

Danny thought about this for a second and realised he'd never thought about it before. He wanted to be Zac Hanaway, definitely, but a real job? Being a grown-up? No idea!

'Dunno,' muttered Danny. 'Something exciting with lots of money, probably!'

The children had arrived at Clootie Bay. The clouds had thinned and the sun was peeping out, sparkling on the water. Danny paused on the soft white sand at the top of the beach. Thick wet seaweed clung to the rocks at the water's edge, glistening in a rainbow of mustard, red and wine-gum green. Tiny birds darted between the silver birch trees edging the shore. Danny breathed in – the salty air tingled in his nose. Like his mum had said, it *was* really beautiful here. Criminally boring, but really beautiful.

He pointed to a small, rocky island just offshore.

'See that island?' he said to Susie. 'I'm going out to it.'

'How?' Susie asked. 'It's cut off by water and you don't have a boat.'

But Danny wasn't listening. He ran to the shore and then waded towards the island in his wellies. He had only got a short way out by the time water started lapping over the top of them.

'Maybe at low tide I could make it,' he said, after plodding back to Susie.

'Low tide is in ...' she checked her watch. 'Approximately two hours and twelve minutes, but even at low tide that island is still cut off.'

Susie was right. The island was always cut off. Danny knew that. He just didn't *want* to know that he knew that. It didn't fit with having an adventure, and having an adventure was his number-one top priority.

'Did you know there was a shipwreck there?' said Danny. 'Granny Flora just told me.'

'The Dutch ship? It was just a small vessel, with only a handful of crew, on its way back from the Indian Ocean,' said Susie. 'The wreckage will have been washed away by now.'

With that, she pulled a science magazine out of her backpack, sat down on the sand and started to read.

Washed away by now, chuntered Danny in his head. *What rubbish!* He wasn't having that. That island was littered with exciting shipwreck goodies – rubies as big as your fist, swords, golden plates and silver cups – he knew it, *and* he knew that he was going to find it all. He just hadn't worked out how yet …

'Why don't you swim out there?' Susie suggested, not looking up from her reading.

Danny's shoulders tensed. He couldn't swim. But he wasn't going to tell Susie that …

'I need a boat,' he said. 'So I can bring back all the swag.'

'Impossible,' she said, still not looking up from her science mag. 'There is a no-lending-boats-to-outsiders rule in Kinoussie. It's been in place for centuries. No one would even consider lending a boat to you, Danny. You're not from round here.'

'But my mum was brought up in Kinoussie!' he protested.

'Not good enough,' Susie replied. 'Forget it. *I* could borrow a boat, but *you* will never be able to.'

Danny poked at the sand with a stick. He might have quite liked to poke Susie too; pop her know-it-all bubble. Her endless logic was making his dream of exciting shipwrecked treasure and adventure slip through his fingers like barely set jelly. He sighed. Next to him, Susie closed her magazine neatly on her lap. The two children stared out to sea silently.

'Shall we go home?' Danny asked. 'I can show you some of my Zac Hanaway comics if you like. Have you heard of Zac Hanaway?'

Susie shrugged. 'I tend to read non-fiction.'

'Hmm,' said Danny. He had a feeling she might say that.

Then he glanced at Susie's magazine lying in her lap. There was a picture of a huge full moon on the cover and the headline read: 'Spring Tides Explained – We explore the science behind these super-low tides.'

He pointed at it with his stick. 'Look!'

'Oh yes,' said Susie. 'Well, a spring tide is just a very, very low tide, caused by the Sun,

Moon and Earth all lining up.'

'When's the next one?' Danny asked.

Susie ran her finger down a chart in the magazine.

'At 10 p.m. on the 29th,' she said.

'That's today!!' said Danny, his eyes wide. 'Tonight! No way! This is amazing!'

'Yes, well, this kind of tidal event is certainly fascinating ...'

'No! Don't you see?' Danny interrupted. 'A really low tide is great for just one reason.'

Susie looked up from the magazine.

'What?' she asked.

'It means that I will be able to walk out to that island!' said Danny. 'To shipwreck island! At last, an adventure. Woo-hoo! Bring! It! On!'

Then Danny gave Susie an excited slap on the shoulder and ran off to lob pebbles into the sea.

Chapter 3

WEE JIMMIE

When the children arrived back at Granny Flora's, there was a white van parked in the yard. On the side, it said: *Wee Jimmie's Odd Jobs*.

A tall, broad man with a green woolly hat and dirty white overalls was talking to Granny Flora. They were pointing up at the roof of the farmhouse.

'That's Wee Jimmie,' Susie whispered.

'He's not wee, he's huge!' said Danny.

'I know. He's the new handyman. Arrived up here about six months ago from Glasgow,' she said.

'Wow, he actually chose to come and live here. Why?' Danny said.

'He says he was looking for the simple life,

away from the big city. Just him and his little dog, Shirley,' said Susie. 'What's wrong with that? Anyway, he's a good handyman. Everyone loves him.'

Danny stared at the gigantic man. He had small eyes with an intense, slightly angry look about them. Why would anyone leave a bustling city like Glasgow to live in a tiny, quiet, remote village? It didn't make sense to Danny.

'Why don't you go and say hello,' said Susie. 'Don't be scared now … I know he's massive! Oh and *make sure you have a look at his hands*!'

The letters WWZD – standing for What Would Zac Do? – flashed across Danny's brain. How his favourite comic hero would act in any given situation was always a useful guide.

'I'll do better than that,' he said, jutting out his chin. 'I'll shake Wee Jimmie's hand.'

Danny ran over to his granny. The two grown-ups were discussing the gutters as Wee Jimmie positioned a huge ladder against the side of the house. Inside the van, a tiny chihuahua stood on the dashboard, yip-yapping at Danny.

'I'm really grateful for this, Jimmie,' Granny Flora was saying. 'I can't have Roddy going up there, he's too wobbly at his age. Now, can I get you anything? Tea? Porridge?'

'Hello!' said Danny.

'Ah, this is my grandson, Danny, here for the holidays,' Granny Flora said.

'Pleased to meet you,' said Danny, thrusting out his hand.

Wee Jimmie's vast, meaty paw closed completely around Danny's tiny, pale hand, like a blue whale swallowing krill. Danny noticed the word LOVE tattooed across the knuckles.

'Pleased to meet you, fella,' said Wee Jimmie. 'I hope you're not going to cause trouble for your granny now.'

He stepped a bit closer to Danny, but reached past him to rap against the van windscreen.

'Quiet, Shirley!' he shouted.

The tiny dog stopped yapping and hopped down on to the driver's seat, looking sulky.

Danny was only half listening. He was focusing on Wee Jimmie's left hand and clearly saw that across the knuckles the word HAT was tattooed in crisp blue ink.

'LOVE and HAT? What the flapjacks does that mean?' Danny asked Susie, when the pair were inside, munching biscuits around the kitchen table, listening to the scraping sound of Wee Jimmie clearing the gutters.

'Well, my personal theory is that he meant to have the word HATE tattooed on to his hand, as it's the opposite of LOVE, but something happened and the tattoo was never finished,' said Susie.

'LOVE and HATE,' said Danny. 'That makes sense. If it was me, I'd have

PORRIDGE, which is for hate, and TARAMASALATA, which is for love.'

Susie wrinkled her nose. 'You'd never fit all those letters on,' she said.

'I wonder why Wee Jimmie never got his tattoo finished?' said Danny.

Susie shrugged.

'Of course, we don't know that it was the word HATE he wanted,' she said. 'It could have been something else.'

'Aye!' laughed Roddy from his corner.

Danny and Susie both nearly jumped out of their seats.

'Crumbs, Roddy,' Danny gasped. 'Didn't see you there!'

'Aye,' said Roddy.

'What do you think about Wee Jimmie?' Danny asked. 'Everyone says he's a nice bloke. Would he want the word HATE on his hand?'

'Aye,' said Roddy, sounding a bit uncertain.

'Maybe the word was meant to be THAT not HATE,' said Susie.

'Or HATS?' said Danny.

'Aye,' said Roddy, shaking his head in a 'don't be ridiculous' kind of way.

'I know, how about WHAT? Or HATO or HATU or, er, CHAT?' Danny suggested.

'LOVE and CHAT,' laughed Susie. 'Yeah, who doesn't like love and chat?'

Danny giggled, then asked, 'Is it HATI?'

'HATI?' laughed Susie. 'What's HATI?'

'Isn't that his dog's name?' said Danny.

'SHIRLEY!!' said Susie. 'His dog's called Shirley, not Hati!'

The two children began laughing uncontrollably now, with Susie muttering 'Hati' between fits of giggles, and it was at this moment that Danny became aware of an almost unbelievable fact. Things were actually happening on the first day at his granny's house! He had wished for some kind of adventure, for stuff to happen, and now it was. A new handyman with HATE possibly tattooed on to his hand had moved into the area – new! Danny was (whisper it) actually getting along with Susie – new! And, double triple joy, there was an island littered with shipwrecked treasure to be explored, this very evening when the tide would be super low. New! New! New! It wasn't quite Zac Hanaway's space adventures, but it wasn't bad either.

Chapter 4

ISLAND

Danny spent the rest of the afternoon imagining how he would stride over to the island, marching through the waves, and then scoop up armfuls of treasure. He would have pockets stuffed with gems and a giant sword hanging from his belt. He'd look amazing! And be rich enough to book that brilliant holiday with his mum and dad! What's not to like?

By evening, the sky was clear and the moon was full. Danny snuck out of the house and ran to Clootie Bay. The tide was definitely really low, but the shipwreck island still looked worryingly far off. Danny was determined though. He turned on his torch, held it above his head and began wading out. Within a few steps, the water was lapping over the top of his wellies, weighing his feet down. WWZD? What Would Zac Do? Not wear wellies, of course! Doh! Stupid mistake! Wobbling, Danny yanked them off and lobbed them on to the beach. He carried on. The water was getting deeper; up to his thighs, now his belt, now nipping at his ribs. *Don't panic*, thought Danny. *Don't think about the fact that you can't swim. Keep going! Think about the treasure!*

He pushed forward through the chilly water. Did something just brush past his belly, below the surface? Danny gasped in shock! He began to run now, only the water pulled him back, slowed him down. On he went, through the waves, imagining huge fish and giant sea snakes with sharp teeth swirling around him, about to bite, when, suddenly, the water level dropped. It was below his ribs, then below his belly button. He had passed the deepest point! Yes!

As the sea became shallower, Danny took bigger and bigger strides, the water dragging at his long legs until he finally tumbled free of its liquid grip and fell down, exhausted, on the shore. He'd done it! He lay there, panting, staring up. A plane blinked its way across the sky.

'Flight MRU 3–96 to Mauritius,' Danny whispered. It was famous in Kinoussie for being the only plane that ever flew over the village. It could be seen at the same time every night, just before 10 p.m.

'So, that means I have about ten minutes to explore, before the tide cuts me off,' Danny said. Somehow, speaking out loud gave him courage. He was shaking with cold. Wow, having an adventure was kind of nerve-wracking. His trembling fingers set the timer on his watch and then he began to climb up on to the island.

Danny's torch picked out his way, through

steep rocks towards a grassy summit. He was looking for a glint, a sparkle, anything that suggested treasure. Gold would be nice, jewels would be exciting! A handful of diamonds? A fat emerald?

He searched the grass but found nothing, then carefully began picking his way down the far side of the island, hopping between rocks, hearing the water lapping deep below. Eventually, he came to another small beach, which faced out to the open ocean, and began scanning the sand for treasure. Still nothing. Not even washed-up timber or sea-ripped rigging. Nothing to hint at a shipwreck. Perhaps Susie was right – it had all been washed away by now. It had been years ago, after all. He checked his watch. Three minutes left until he had to leave. No! There had to be treasure here! He didn't want his dream of an adventure to be over yet.

Danny moved further up the small beach, then spotted a low cave at the end. He edged nearer, then stopped. There were prints in the sand, leading into the cave. He shone the torch on them. They were a bird's footprints. The hairs on Danny's neck prickled a little. These prints were huge! Perhaps from a seagull. No, they weren't webbed like a seabird's feet. Maybe an eagle? On the beach? That didn't feel right. Maybe …

SQUAWK!

Danny froze.

'Who's there?' he said, his voice wobbling.

He darted the torch up towards the cave mouth – and gasped! An eye shone back. A tiny golden eye, staring angrily.

Danny dared not move. He could feel his heart thumping in his chest. The eye stared out at him, unblinking. He gripped the torch extra hard. The beam bounced around,

but he could also see a narrow face. It had skin, and feathers. And a beak! A huge hooked beak, greenish towards the tip. Danny moved the torch a little more. The creature was big too. He thought it might come up to his waist. He bit his lip; the eye stared back. Nobody moved until, suddenly …

BEEP BEEP BEEP BEEP! The alarm on his watch ripped through the silence. The creature squawked again in terror, Danny screamed, tripped backwards and dropped his torch. It hit a stone and clicked off. He fell to his knees, fumbling for the light. It had to be here somewhere ... Then he looked up. Where was the creature now? Danny peered through the watery moonlight. Where was it? It had moved. His ears strained. He could hear a rustling sound, a soft step on the sand. Was it nearby? Was it coming for him?

Zac Hanaway would never panic or run, but Zac was far from Danny's mind now as he tore along the beach and clambered awkwardly up the rocks, with only the pale moonlight to guide him. Back on the grassy summit, he stopped for a second, his lungs bursting. Was that the creature on the beach below, still staring at him with its golden eyes? Danny didn't stick around to check. The tide was coming in and he didn't fancy being marooned here for the night with a mysterious mad-eyed monster. He turned and ran, thundering down the rocky side of the island, ripping his socks and scraping his feet on barnacles. Then he plunged back into the sea, wincing as the saltwater hit his cuts and grazes, and began wading with night-marishly slow strides through the water (come on, come on, come on) until he was safely back on dry land.

Danny ran up the beach before collapsing down, panting and shaking. He stared back at the island as the tide rushed in and the water around it got deeper. His left foot was grazed and painful, his clothes were soaked and he was shivering with fear and cold. But as he pulled on his wellies and turned to limp back through the trees to Granny Flora's house, he also felt more alive and excited than he'd ever felt before. He hadn't found treasure, but he had found *something*. What was it? As he trudged home, he could only find one explanation for that squat, grey creature with beady eyes and a hooked beak. But no, surely not. It couldn't be, could it?

Chapter 5

RETURN

Danny stole quietly back into the house, but lay awake in his bed, twitchy and excited. Thoughts were rattling around his brain, like pennies in a washing machine. He couldn't believe what he'd just seen on the island. He replayed those moments on the beach – the torchlight, the beady eye, that creature! – but couldn't be sure what he'd seen. Was it dangerous? Did it have a taste for ten-year-old-boy flesh? Danny winced under the blankets. Perhaps he should forget about it; leave well alone. But how could he? Something was happening at last. In Kinoussie! Unheard of! It was something to tell Cal and all his friends about when he got home. It was as exciting as the time Zac

Hanaway discovered a whole city populated by mythical aquatic meerkats, living beneath the seas of Minto 9. As Danny drifted off to sleep just one thought went through his mind – he had to go back!

All plans to return to the island were briefly interrupted when Danny got up the next morning – and screamed! His foot! Gah! The grazes from clattering down the rocks last night were stinging like salt on a slug. Granny Flora rushed into the room.

'It's the rough floorboards under the bed,' Danny spluttered, quickly cooking up an excuse for his poorly foot. 'I just scraped against them.'

'Rough boards?' said Granny Flora. 'That won't do. I'll get Wee Jimmie to look at that.'

'At my foot?' Danny asked, worried. He didn't fancy the handyman manhandling him.

'No, you daftie, at the floorboards,' she

said. 'Here, come into the bathroom.'

Granny Flora carefully wrapped up Danny's sore foot, padding it with a bandage, and was just tidying away the first-aid box when there was a 'Hello?' from downstairs. (No one ever knocked in Kinoussie.)

Susie? Danny wondered; more than wondered, in fact. He *hoped* it was her. He realised that hoping to see Susie was highly unusual, but this summer at Granny's was proving unusual in every way so far. He wanted to ask her something.

The 'hello' hadn't come from Susie though, but from Moira MacNair, known by everyone as Moira Storm, because she was always looking at the sky, sniffing the air and predicting when the weather would turn for the worst. Moira was only sixty but she looked eighty. Her back was bent over, like a tree shaped by the wind. Though weirdly, she

43

could still ride a bike, her forehead almost brushing the handlebars. This is how she had arrived at Granny Flora's farm.

'I'll be down presently,' Granny Flora shouted. 'Danny, go and say morning to Moira. I'm driving her into Fort Plother for the dentist. I just need to brush my hair.'

Danny hobbled downstairs reluctantly. Moira Storm gave him the willies.

'Ah, you're here, are ye?' she said. Then her eyes fell to his bandaged foot.

'Hurt yourself?' she asked.

'Just a graze,' Danny said.

'Up to no good, I'll be bound,' muttered Moira. 'Young boys like you are always looking for trouble. There will be trouble enough when the storm blows in later.'

'It's sunny though,' said Danny.

'FOR NOW!' Moira said in a loud, doomy voice.

Luckily, Granny Flora appeared at this point and whisked Moira out through the front door. Danny watched them leave and then raced round to Susie's house in the village. He ran past Sheila Creasy's neat white house – she was sitting on a bench outside smoking a tiny pipe, waiting to lure a passer-by in so she could talk about the old days. He waved and ran on, past the Spar shop where a sign outside said **TURNIPS – BUY ONE, GET ONE FREE, WHILE STOCKS LAST!** and on past the bus shelter where Jamie Dunoon often sat, waiting for a bus that never came, as no bus had stopped in Kinoussie for twelve years. Then up the path past the squat, low church, on past Scotland's smallest campsite, to a row of cottages where Susie lived.

Susie came to the door.

'I need to borrow a boat,' Danny puffed.

'Impossible,' she said. 'There is a rule that ...'

'Yes, yes, I know,' said Danny impatiently. 'OK, I need *you* to borrow a boat!'

'So you can go on to that island?' Susie asked.

'Yes.'

'In search of treasure?' she snorted. 'You've been reading too many Jack Getaway comics!'

'Zac Hanaway,' muttered Danny. 'Anyway – I'm not looking for treasure. Not any more. There's something on the island. I went out there last night when the tide was really low and saw it.'

'What kind of something?' Susie asked.

'A, er, creature,' he said. 'I dunno, I didn't get a good look at it, but it had a beak and it squawked. I want to go back there, when it's not dark.'

'So, you saw a seagull and now you want to row out there so you can see it in daylight,' said Susie.

'It wasn't a seagull,' Danny said, feeling cross. 'Way bigger, with a big hooked beak!'

'An overweight seagull?' Susie offered.

'No!' Danny shouted. 'Look, come with me if you don't believe me!'

He hadn't quite planned to invite Susie to share his new discovery, but he was desperate to get back to the island and she was his only chance.

'Oh, come on, science girl, don't you want to discover a new species?' Danny said. 'You do, don't you? I know you're tempted. What would, I dunno, Chris Packham do?'

Susie paused, considering this. 'Fine, I'll get you a boat. Just give me an hour,' she said. 'Then we take a quick look and come straight back. There's a programme about

48

the lifecycle of tapeworms on the radio this afternoon. I can't miss it.'

'Great! I'll bring supplies,' Danny said.

'Look, this isn't some jolly scout-camp picnic!' Susie said. 'We go, we take a look, we get back in time for tapeworms.'

'I'll bring supplies,' Danny said again, but Susie had shut the door in his face.

Chapter 6

DISCOVERY

Susie called Danny and told him to meet her at Murdo McMurdo's house, not far from Clootie Bay. He had a little rowing boat that he'd agreed to lend her. He was family – her mum's uncle's second cousin – and besides, he owed Susie a favour after she managed to get a dead mouse out from behind his oven, using only Silly Putty, a bread knife and a hairdryer.

'Wait in the bushes until he's gone back inside,' said Susie. 'He'll go nuts if he finds out that an outsider is going in his boat.'

From Danny's hideout on the edge of the garden, he thought Murdo looked a bit like a wild boar. Short, dark, wiry whiskers on the sides of his face, tiny eyes. Murdo pointed to a small building in the woods back from the shore and, once he'd gone inside, Susie beckoned Danny over.

It wasn't easy lugging the boat down the beach. Danny's foot was sore and his backpack was heavy, plus Susie kept complaining about the way he was holding the boat. He was creating drag, apparently. What did that even mean? Once they were in the boat, progress through the calm water was easier. Susie paddled effortlessly.

'Let's head for the far side,' said Danny. 'That's where I saw ... it!'

Within minutes, they were at the island's tiny bay Danny had discovered the night before. He scanned the beach for footprints, but the tide had been in and out since he last visited; the sand looked like it had been ironed.

The children hopped down from the boat.

Susie wandered off while Danny approached the cave. In the sunshine, he could see it clearly. It was low and cramped but stretched deep into the dark rock. Could anything live in here?

Danny stopped, just steps away from the cave mouth. There was no sign of life, no sign of anything. Had it all been a dream? Was he so desperate to live like Zac Hanaway and have an adventure that his mind had made one up?

Then, Danny heard a movement from the darkness – a soft rustle, then a **click-clack** sound. He froze. Silence again, except for the lapping of the waves behind him. He peered into the cave, not daring to move. He couldn't see anything, so why was his skin suddenly rippling with goosebumps? Because he was being *watched*, he knew it. Another faint rustling sound and then, finally, Danny saw it. That eye! That same eye his torch had picked out last night. Small, golden, eager. From the dim, dark cave it stared out, unblinking, unafraid.

His heart pumping, Danny crouched down slowly and eased his backpack off his shoulders. Without taking his gaze off the eye, he reached inside and found a cracker.

'Here!' he whispered. 'Food. Nice crispy cracker. Want one?'

He held the cracker out, his hand shaking. The eye stared and stared. Then a rasping squawk thundered out of the cave, amplified by its low ceiling.

Danny hurled the cracker like a Frisbee, and fell backwards in terror. Quick as a grey flash, a stocky bird rushed out of the dark cave and, with a beat of its stubby wings, jumped into the air and caught the cracker perfectly in its leathery, hooked beak.

It held the cracker there for a split second, as if to say, 'Good catch, eh?' Then it crunched it up, sending out a shower of crumbs from each side of its beak.

'Un-*real*!' Danny whispered, still staring. He couldn't believe what he was looking at – what he had discovered. The bird stood dead still and eyed him back.

'Squawk!'

Danny flinched with shock. Yikes, that squawk was loud! The bird trotted back and forth a little, its beak open, its eyes fiery. Danny sat rooted to the spot, terrified any movement would scare the creature away. He let out a laugh, then quickly covered his mouth with his hand, before the bird was startled. His heart nearly burst, like it was having some kind of cardiac sugar rush. Why? Because this creature standing in front of him was extraordinary. It was amazing. It was unbelievable ...

It was a dodo.

Chapter 7

DECISION

'Danny! Danny!'

Susie was racing down the cliff above Danny, like a mountain goat running for the bus.

'I cannot believe what I've just found!' she said, holding something up as she hopped down, eyes glued to the uneven rocks.

'Look, look,' she said, running along the beach towards Danny. He stood up now, his tall body hiding the dodo.

Panting, Susie stopped in front of him and spread out her hands, talking feverishly. 'It's the skull of a bird, quite a big one too, and just look at this beak. It's so unusual! I just can't think what kind of bird this is though, it's not like anything I've ever ...'

'Squawk!'

Susie stopped.

'What was that?' she asked.

Danny didn't turn to see the yellowish, leathery face with its gigantic bulbous beak peep out from behind him. He didn't have to. He was looking at Susie's expression, which said it all. Her mouth dropped open, her head shook.

The dodo stepped out from behind Danny and stood next to him. Its yellow eyes looked at Susie and blinked. It clacked its beak once, as if to say hello.

'What?' spluttered Susie in a whisper. 'Is. It?'

'It's a dodo, Susie. Look at it!' said Danny.

'Impossible!' she said. 'Extinct! They are all extinct. As dead as … !'

She waved the skeleton head at Danny. It

was clearly the skull of a dodo. The living bird stared at it too.

'Those have to be dodo bones,' said Danny. 'Probably means there was more than one living here, at some point, perhaps a whole family. What do you think?'

Susie shook her head frantically, neat curtains of straight hair swinging from side to side. The bird looked between the two children, then pecked at Danny's bag.

'Careful!' screeched Susie, leaping backwards. 'It's after your bag! Watch the beak!'

'It's hungry, I think,' said Danny.

He pulled the rest of the crackers out of his backpack and scattered them in front of the bird, keeping his hands away from that beak. It *was* pretty scary. It must have been over twenty centimetres long.

Quickly and greedily the bird pecked up the crackers, munching eagerly, showering the beach with crumbs. Danny gazed at the bird as it ate, tsunamis of happiness crashing over him. Feeding a dodo! Feeding it crackers! Shut up!

Then Danny started to look more closely at the bird, at the gaps where feathers were missing, at its scraggy tail and flat chest. Weren't dodos meant to be plump? It held one clawed foot awkwardly off the sand, as though it were painful.

'I wonder what there is to eat here? Or drink?' he said. 'It was sheltering in that cave, which must be freezing. That foot looks sore too. It needs looking after.'

The dodo finished the last of the crackers and stood there, blinking slowly, digesting the food, perhaps its first proper meal in a while.

Slowly, reality started to seep into Danny's happy brain. Reality was like that; it never went away for long. He had found a dodo – joy of joys! The adventure he'd longed for! At last! But what was he going to do now? *I have to bring it more food, perhaps some blankets for its cave, and a bucket of fresh water,* he thought. That would mean borrowing the boat, and not once, but lots of times, to keep the dodo supplied. *That won't work!* Murdo McMurdo would get suspicious. Then Danny remembered how hard it had been to lug the boat down to Clootie Bay. He would have to get Susie's help each time, and Susie was … Hang on, where was she?

'We need to go!' Susie shouted. She was down by the boat. 'Tapeworm programme, remember?'

Danny raced down the beach to her.

'What are you doing?' he asked. 'We can't just turn our backs on it!'

'Yes we can,' said Susie sharply, 'because it doesn't exist. Dodos died out, so this isn't a dodo, it's just a thing. An escaped turkey or a vulture or a very big pigeon or, or … I don't know! But it can't be a dodo. They're all gone. I've read about them in books.'

'Well, forget about books!' Danny exploded. 'This is real. Right here, in front of your eyes! It needs help. Look at it!'

The children looked back at the beach, where the dodo was busy snuffling in Danny's backpack for food. It jerked its head up, and the backpack fell down, covering its face and neck like a bulky balaclava with straps. A pot of Danny's beloved taramasalata plopped on to the sand.

'It's hungry, see?' he said. The bird was now trying to reverse out of the bag, but kept butting into rocks. Muffled squawks came from inside the bag.

'Stupid, more like,' muttered Susie.

Danny ran back to the bird.

'You numpty!' he laughed. He carefully lifted the bag off.

The dodo blinked in the light, then spotted the pot of pink fishy dip and pecked excitedly at it. Danny took the lid off and the bird plunged its beak into the pot, its eyes sparkling.

'Delicious, isn't it?' Danny said.

'Come on, Danny, we have to go!' Susie shouted. She had her life jacket on now, ready. 'Come on! We need to leave NOW! Tapeworm programme! Leave the turkey and let's go!'

The bird gazed calmly at Danny, barely blinking. Danny stared back, at its scruffy body and bent foot, and then at its eyes. They were bright, questioning eyes. He felt they stared right into him, waiting for answers.

'Danny, NOW!' shouted Susie.

Danny remained rooted to the spot.

'OK, fine. Have it your way. See you later, Danny!'

Susie pushed the boat off the sand and into the shallows.

'Bye then! I'm going now. Have a nice life!' she yelled.

Danny watched as Susie jumped into the boat and grabbed the oars with an angry flick of her hair. 'Enjoy your feathered friend!' she muttered furiously. 'Maybe you can eat it when your taramasa-splatter runs out!'

Danny looked at the bird, then at Susie beginning to paddle away.

'WAIT!' he shouted.

Quickly, Danny took his hoodie off, threw it around the bird and zipped it up. Then, taking one of the empty sleeves, he gently led the bird down to the shore, like he was walking a two-legged, feathery dog.

'Just hold on a second,' he said to Susie. 'I'm bringing it with us!'

'You're doing WHAT?' she screamed.

'I can hide it in the outbuilding at Granny's,' said Danny. 'It's fine.'

'Are you mad?' spluttered Susie. 'Don't answer that, I already know. Yes! The answer is, yes you are. You want to lug an overgrown chicken back to your gran's house and hide it! Are you completely bonkers?'

'I don't want to leave it here,' said Danny. 'It's too special to leave here. Too amazing. I'm going to bring it back!'

'Wait!' said Susie, poking the oar against Danny's chest like a sword, stopping him on the shore. 'Number one, this is not a dodo, because it cannot be a dodo. And number two, how do you know it wants to come with you? Has it not occurred to you that this is its home?'

'This isn't its home!' Danny snorted. 'It's just somewhere it's ended up, just like I end up in Kinoussie every summer. Doesn't mean

I want to be here! I wish someone would come along and rescue me.'

He shoved the oar aside and led the dodo into the shallows.

'This is madness. You haven't thought about this properly, Danny,' Susie said. 'How are you even going to get it into the boat? Ask it nicely?'

'That's not a bad idea!' said Danny. He crouched next to the dodo.

'Hello, Mr Dodo,' he said.

'Or Ms!' Susie tutted.

'I'm not going to hurt you,' Danny went on. 'I'm going to take you home where it's safe and warm with lots of nice porridge to eat. What am I saying? Porridge is horrid, but there are tons of crackers there and nice cheese and my own private supply of tara-masalata. All you have to do is hop up into this boat.'

The dodo stared. Susie shook her head. Danny tapped the side of the boat and did a little jump, demonstrating what to do. The dodo tilted its head, looking quizzically at him.

'Just hop on in!' Danny said. 'Come on. Up you get.'

The dodo stood still for several seconds and then calmly walked towards the boat. Using its beak as a grip, it raised one huge yellow foot towards the side of the boat, but couldn't quite hook it over the top. Danny cupped his hands to make a little step. The dodo understood. It placed its good foot on Danny's hand, pushed off, bounced upwards and tumbled into the boat, knocking Susie over. She fell flat on her back and lay there, with the dodo standing on her chest, pinning her down. It stared at her, its beak almost touching the tip of her nose. She dared not blink.

Then, with a little flap of its short wings, the bird simply hopped off.

Susie sat up, breathing heavily and clutching the oar across her chest like a weapon as Danny pushed the boat out to sea.

'Give it your life jacket,' he told her.

'It's extinct already!' said Susie. 'Why does it get to wear a life jacket?'

'I can't give it mine,' said Danny, hopping into the boat. 'I can't swim!'

'Oh, this just gets better!' Susie said, ripping off her life jacket and handing it to Danny. He secured it around the dodo and the unlikely party set off back around the island: a fuming girl on the oars, a beaming boy in the bow and, sitting between them, a dodo wearing a hoodie and a life jacket with smears of pink taramasalata around its yellow beak.

Chapter 8

HIDE

Back onshore, Danny frowned. Susie was right – he hadn't thought about this properly. All he had known was that he wanted that dodo. He wanted to feed it, play with it, have it as his own supercool companion all summer long, for massive adventures and nutty fun – Danny and his dodo. Not even in his maddest dreams could he have cooked up this idea for his summer holiday. Wow! How totally awesome!

Except, here was reality again, crashing the party ... How was Danny going to transport a large dodo back to Granny's? It was a five-minute walk, at least, and the dodo's foot was sore. Plus, what if someone spotted them? He had to keep this bird secret and safe, for now anyway. If anyone saw it, the word would be round Kinoussie faster than butter melting in a hot frying pan. There were no secrets in Kinoussie, after all.

Then Danny spied an old wheelbarrow, upturned in the trees.

'We'll move him in that,' he said.

'We?' Susie spluttered.

'Please!' Danny said. 'We'll leave the life jacket and hoodie on as a disguise.'

He tipped the wheelbarrow on to its side and together the two children scooped the dodo into it and set it upright. The bird seemed tired now and a little nervous. It sat, hunched, bouncing awkwardly when Danny and Susie pushed it over a bump. They paused at the entrance to the farmyard and Danny checked no one was around. The coast was clear. Granny Flora was still out with Moira Storm. Everything seemed quiet. Quickly, he wheeled the bird over to the outbuilding and pulled open the red doors.

'Just a second, wait here!' he said to Susie, before diving inside.

She peered in after him. The outbuilding was stuffed to the rafters with junk. There were garden tools, a rusty beach umbrella, a broken desk covered in plant pots, boxes filled with who knew what, and a suitcase of jam jars, each one full of rusty screws and washers. There was an armchair with a missing foot, slumped to one side. Further back, Susie spotted a huge tower of old newspapers, a trumpet, what had to be the basket of a hot-air balloon, a pram, a shop mannequin wearing a top hat and at least twelve buckets.

Danny was hastily clearing a path through all this rubbish towards the furthest corner. Here, there was a low wall with a neat cubbyhole behind; perhaps a place to store logs or

coal once upon a time. This, he quickly decided, would be the dodo's home. He ran back to the bird, helped it out of the wheelbarrow and ushered it in, like he was showing it to a hotel room.

The dodo stood in the cubbyhole and stared quietly at Danny.

'You stay here,' he said, holding his hand up in a stop sign.

'Here!' he added, pointing into the cubbyhole.

'I bring you food.' Then he did an eating with a knife and fork motion, and rubbed his tummy.

'Oh please!' Susie moaned. 'I'm pretty sure that if this is a dodo, which it can't be, by the way, as we have already established, but if it *is*, then it doesn't understand what a knife and fork is.'

'It understands all right,' said Danny. 'It's

like Roddy Aye. Granny always says you can understand him through his ayes *and* his eyes. Look at its eyes! They're intelligent. It understands me!'

'Glad someone does,' Susie sighed. 'Not sure I do. Oh what have I become? I usually understand *everything*!'

'Look, it's not hard!' said Danny. 'This is a dodo and it's going to stay here for now.'

'Then what?' said Susie. 'Danny?'

He was busy spreading an old picnic rug he'd found on the floor of the cubbyhole. Eventually, he looked up and saw Susie's worried face.

'Look, it's fine,' said Danny. 'It's more than fine. It's the adventure of a lifetime – my lifetime!'

Susie shook her head.

'Well, I don't happen to like adventures – you never know quite how they'll turn out. I like fact, science and books. I like programmes about tapeworms.'

She glanced at her watch.

'And I'm missing one right now! Noooo!'

With that, Susie ran out of the outbuilding.

'Don't mind her,' Danny said to the dodo. 'She's just having her head blown off by you! She'll get over it. Now, how about some lunch?'

A minute later, he stood in his granny's larder, a small room off the kitchen, where she kept all her food. He scanned the shelves. What did dodos like to eat? He didn't know. Crackers and taramasalata, yes. Rice? Tinned peaches? A cold sausage? Some leftover baked beans in a coffee cup? Danny just grabbed what was portable and stuffed it into his backpack. He raced back across the kitchen, heading for the front door, then for the second time that day, he had the strong sense that someone was staring at him.

'Oh, hi, Roddy!' he said, finally spotting the old man sitting in the shadows by the fire, his knitting in his lap. 'Didn't see you there.'

'Aye,' said Roddy, gazing calmly at Danny, with just the hint of a smile.

'Just getting ready for a picnic!' Danny lied. 'Me and Susie. Off for a nice picnic some- where outdoors ...'

'Aye,' said Roddy, nodding.

Back in the outbuilding, Danny arranged the food on an old, rusty tray and passed it to the dodo. It ate greedily. Its beak tapping the metal tray sounded like rain on a car roof. Danny grinned as the bird grabbed each cheese slice, each Hula Hoop, each custard cream! When the tray was empty, it shuffled impatiently on the spot.

'All right, calm down, greedy!' Danny giggled. 'Now, how about a drink?'

He mimed taking a cup, lifting it to his lips and swallowing. The dodo ruffled its stubby wings and clacked its beak.

Danny filled an old metal bucket from the water butt by the doors. The dodo took long swigs from it, tipping its head back as the cool water trickled down its throat.

'You absolute beauty,' Danny said. 'You're just so amazing.'

The dodo carried on drinking.

'You're so incredible. In fact, you have just turned my pants holiday into the most awesome holiday I have ever, ever had. We're going to have so much fun together. Just you and me. When I tell my friend Cal about this back home he is going to pee his trousers! Oh, but then there's Susie! Heck! What if she says something? I need to speak to her.'

He pulled his mobile phone out of his pocket. No signal. Of course.

'Don't go away, I just need to make a phone call in the house,' Danny said to the dodo.

He held an imaginary phone to his ear, then realised this was more stupid than a knife and fork. How could a supposedly extinct bird know anything about telecommunications?

He picked his way back through the outhouse and then shut the double doors carefully behind him, spending a few moments securing the handles with a length of rope. No one ever went in the outbuilding, but he still couldn't risk someone finding the precious dodo. Just as he pulled the final knot tight, a shadow fell over him; a huge shadow in the shape of a huge man.

'Hello there, Danny,' said a deep voice.

Danny spun round. Wee Jimmie! He was

glowering over him like a grizzly bear in a green woolly hat, a hammer swinging by his side in the hand that read HAT. Danny had been so wrapped up in feeding the dodo, he hadn't heard Wee Jimmie's van pull into the yard.

'Just been checking over those floorboards under your bed,' Wee Jimmie said, without moving. Danny was pinned against the door. 'Couldn't see anything wrong with them, so I'm wondering how you hurt your foot. You told your gran it was on rough boards, but I'm not so sure, you see?'

Danny gulped and squeezed past Wee Jimmie. Shirley the chihuahua, locked in the van, began yip-yapping at the sight of him.

'I've got delicate feet,' Danny said, cringing a bit at how rubbish this fib was. 'I'm from the South. Weak feet …'

'Hmm,' said Wee Jimmie, as if thinking

this over. 'I'm also wondering what you've been up to in the outbuilding. Last time I checked it was full of junk.'

'It is!' said Danny. 'Totally full. The fullest! But I like exploring in there, you know! I won't do it again though. Too dusty! Upsets my nose. I'm from the South, after all. Weak nose too ...'

'And that leads me to wonder something else,' Wee Jimmie went on, swinging his hammer idly and ignoring Danny's words. 'If it's so full of junk, why would you be tying up the doors so tight? I mean, who would want to go in there? Who would want to *steal* from there? There's no crime in Kinoussie, after all, everyone knows that.'

'It's best to be careful,' said Danny.

'Maybe so,' said Wee Jimmie. 'Your gran could have anything in there, couldn't she, among all the junk. Buried treasure!'

He grinned at Danny.

'Maybe I'll take a look one day. I still have a few contacts in Glasgow who'd be interested in a spot of trade, or a little deal. Could make a few quid,' he said. 'You don't mind, do you?'

Wee Jimmie stared at Danny as his face went from palest pink to full-on boiled gammon. Danny did mind. He knew there really was treasure in there. And it was his and only his! Not gold and silver, but a precious, extinct-yet-alive bird.

Then, suddenly, he felt his shoulder being patted in a most reassuring way. It was Roddy Aye. Roddy then walked up to Wee Jimmie and held out a red woollen hat that he must have just finished knitting.

'For me?' Wee Jimmie asked.

'Aye,' said Roddy.

'Thanks very much!' said Wee Jimmie, looking genuinely pleased.

Shirley yip-yapped from inside the van as Wee Jimmie put down his hammer and pulled off his green woolly hat to reveal a gigantic, shiny bald head. He put on his new red one, patting it happily.

This was Danny's chance to escape. Silently and gratefully, he slipped back into the house.

Chapter 9

FIRST AID

Danny called Susie and made her promise not to say a word about the dodo. She said that she wouldn't anyway, because Danny wasn't hiding a dodo, because dodos had died out over three hundred years ago, because she'd read that and because everyone knew that and because, and because, and because …

Fine. Susie could be a no-no when it came to the dodo if she wanted, although it seemed nuts to Danny. The dodo was alive, real and the most exciting thing that had ever happened, ever, ever, full stop.

That afternoon, once Wee Jimmie had left and Granny was home and grappling with the crossword at the kitchen table, Danny crept back into the outbuilding. The dodo was asleep, its injured foot curled beneath it. It opened one golden eye, then another and then clacked its beak excitedly at Danny. Danny meant food! Food good!

He heaped some food on to the tray and pushed it in front of the dodo, who greedily chomped its way through six dried apricots, a couple of toast crusts, a few more custard creams and a little pot of jelly. As it ate, throwing its head back to gulp down the goodies, its poorly foot hovered awkwardly, only touching the ground for moments at a time.

'Oh, that foot hurts, doesn't it?' said Danny. 'I know how that feels. I once stepped on something in the grass, but I didn't know it, and then I got this big infected sore lump on my foot and it was all full of puss and stuff.'

The dodo blinked at him.

'Anyway. I'll get the first-aid kit.'

The dodo blinked again.

'You know, first aid. It's like help, that you do first. Not second. Never mind. Hang on.'

Danny raced back to the house and opened the cupboard under the bathroom basin. The green box with a red cross on it was back in there, where Granny Flora had put it after patching up his foot.

Back in the outbuilding, Danny realised he had not one single clue how to fix a poorly foot. A poorly *bird's* foot, in fact. A poorly *possibly extinct bird's* foot. He grabbed his phone and tried to search for a useful video on YouTube, but of course, no signal.

The dodo watched as Danny swiped the screen, tilted its head and then pecked the screen sharply.

'No, no, no, you do it like this,' said Danny. 'It's swipe, not peck, swipe not ...'

The dodo darted its beak at the screen again and pecked it hard.

CRACK!

The smooth screen fractured and thousands of tiny lines split across it.

'What! You idiot!' Danny shouted. The dodo jumped in surprise.

'Sorry,' said Danny, 'it's just that was a bit too much. Never mind. Not your fault, I suppose, you're new to phones. I'll just have to tell my mum I dropped it or a giant midge flew into it or something.'

The dodo blinked at him again.

'OK, look, just stay there, don't move, while I get some cream on that foot. That's what Mum always does – a bit of cream on first, then a plaster.'

He squeezed a little blob of white antiseptic cream on to his finger, put the tube down and leaned forward slowly, but the dodo snapped up the tube of cream in its powerful beak and clamped down. **SQUEEZE!** A thick ribbon of cream flew out like Silly String, splatting Danny on the side of his head. He yelped with surprise, like he'd been shot. His hand went up to his face, slapped the trail of cream and squidged it all over his fingers, his palm, the side of his face, his ear, his hair.

'Woah!' laughed Danny. 'Easy there!'

He tried to get the cream off, wiping his hand on the rug and flicking it around angrily, tiny flecks of antiseptic cream flying off as he did. The dodo hopped around awkwardly, and eventually, Danny noticed, stepped clumsily in some cream.

'Good,' he said, 'at least some of it's gone in your cut. I need to get a plaster on that now.'

Danny fumbled with a big plaster. It was hard to get the wrapper off with his greasy, slippery, hospital-smelling fingers. Finally, he reached towards the dodo's foot, but the dodo grabbed the plaster with its beak, where it got stuck. The dodo, peering at it so he nearly went cross-eyed, clacked its beak and shook its head, trying to get it off.

'Stay still, stay still,' said Danny as the dodo flung its head left and right, eventually toppling over. Danny swooped in while the dodo wriggled on the rug, trying to get back up. With a satisfying rip sound, he whipped the plaster off and sat down heavily, panting.

The dodo got back on its feet and ruffled its feathers. Boy and bird looked at each other for a bit, both rattled by this round of first aid.

Danny fumbled another plaster out of its wrapper.

'Now, keep nice and still, and this will all be just fine ...' he said. This time, the dodo turned and dived head first into the corner of the cubbyhole. Danny tried to reach its foot, but the dodo kicked out and this time the plaster ended up stuck firmly in its white, fluffy tail feathers.

'Not again!' said Danny. 'How can putting a plaster on be so hard!'

The dodo spied the plaster in its feathers and tried to grab it, like a dog chasing its tail. It spun around and around, swaying on its unsteady feet, bouncing off the walls of the cubbyhole.

'This is ridiculous!' said Danny, watching the rotating dodo. 'You're the worst patient ever.'

The dodo paused and clacked its beak at him, before hiding its head in the corner again.

Danny yanked the plaster out, pulling a white feather with it. The dodo squawked loudly.

'Sorry!' said Danny.

He sat down in the wobbly armchair, wondering what to do next. That's when he saw the old pram parked over near the door. It had a few old toys – rattles and a string of beads – hanging from its hood; things a baby might like to stare at or grab. This gave Danny an idea.

Quickly, he found one of the jam jars full of

washers and threaded some on to a long piece of string. Then he looped the string over a bamboo cane and put this across the walls of the cubby.

'Ta da!' he said. 'Well, look at it, will you? It's your new toy.'

The dodo looked round. Danny chinked the washers together. They made a nice sound. The dodo began to turn, interested now, and slowly waddled over. It nudged the string nervously, another chinking sound. It did it again, and again, delighted now. This was Danny's chance. He rummaged in the first-aid kit for a bandage. Plasters didn't work; he'd have to wrap the foot up instead. But there was no bandage. Of course, because it was on his own foot. He ripped off his trainer and sock and unwound it.

'Keep playing with those washers, dodo,' he muttered as he slowly took the bird's poorly foot in one hand. He could see a deep graze, and began winding the bandage around it. 'Nice washers, aren't they? Keep playing with the nice washers, that's right ...'

Finally, he tied the bandage and sat back.

'Done! Phew! Not bad!' said Danny, gazing at the dodo's foot. The dodo finally noticed too, and pecked at the fat ball of bandage.

'Don't do that!' said Danny, waving his hands. 'Leave it on, at least until tomorrow.'

The dodo put his sore foot down and, with the bandage padding it, could finally stand. He was a bit lopsided, but it was an improvement.

'Job done – finally!' said Danny. 'Now I think I need some dinner and a lie-down. Enjoy your washers. I'll see you in the morning.'

Chapter 10

PHEW!

Back in the house, Danny put the first-aid kit away then found his granny in the kitchen.

'Ooh you smell, er, now then – how do you smell?' said Granny Flora, looking over at Danny. She leaned in and gave him a kiss.

'You're all greasy!' she said, feeling his creamy antiseptic face.

'Suncream!' said Danny quickly.

'But it's been cloudy this afternoon, and a bit wet,' said Granny Flora.

'Well, best to be careful,' said Danny.

Granny Flora stared at him for a second and then shrugged.

'Lay the table, dinner's almost ready,' she said. 'I thought you were in the outbuilding this afternoon anyway. No sun in there, just junk. I really should clear it. I bet Wee Jimmie would help.'

Danny dropped the forks he was holding on the floor. They hit the tiles with a metallic clatter.

'Careful!' said Granny Flora.

'When?' stuttered Danny.

'When to be careful?' Granny Flora said. 'Just, you know, in general. When handling cutlery or crossing the road, that sort of thing.'

'No, when are you clearing out the out-building?' Danny said.

'Oh that!' said Granny Flora, returning to her stew. 'Some time. Next year maybe. Now pick those forks up off the floor.'

Danny let out a huge sigh of relief as he crouched to gather up the cutlery. For a second he feared Granny and Wee Jimmie would clear the outbuilding and discover the dodo. That must not happen!

'How's the foot?' Granny Flora asked.

Danny looked up sharply and hit his head on the underside of the table.

'Which foot?' he asked, rubbing his head and peering up at his gran.

'The one you hurt on the rough boards, you big ninny!' she laughed. 'You're asking some odd questions tonight, Danny my boy.'

'Oh, I thought you meant … doesn't matter,' he said, feeling relief wash over him.

'What other foot would I be talking about?' she said, staring at her grandson.

Oh, just the foot of the dodo I rescued who is living in the outbuilding, Danny thought. *That other foot!*

'Show me,' said Granny Flora.

Danny took his sock off.

'Where's the bandage I put on it?' asked Granny Flora.

'Er,' said Danny, trying to think up a good reason why it was no longer on his foot.

'Let me at least get a plaster on that instead,' said Granny Flora. She went upstairs for the first-aid kit. When she came back down to the kitchen she looked confused.

'Danny! Have you had the plasters? There were plenty in there the other day. And the antiseptic cream is almost all used up. What's going on?'

'I was playing, with Susie,' he lied, quickly.

'Doctors and nurses. Sorry. I'll buy you some more plasters, promise!'

'Doctors and nurses? At your age? I thought you preferred your phones,' she said.

'It's broken,' said Danny, then wished he hadn't. 'I dropped it on a rock.'

'Oh dear, what next?' said Granny Flora. 'Your mother won't be pleased. And I suppose it was you and Susie who brought that wheelbarrow here. The one I found over near the outbuilding.'

Danny's eyes pinged wide. Had Granny Flora seen them pushing the dodo earlier?

'Ambulance,' he squeaked, another fib tumbling off his tongue. 'We were pretending it was an ambulance in our game of doctors and, er, yeah …'

'I'm guessing you found it down by the beach,' she said.

That's exactly where we found it, thought

Danny. *Oh pancakes, she's on to me. She's seen the dodo …*

'It'll be one of Willy McNeish's, no doubt,' said Granny Flora, smiling fondly. 'Poor old Willy is so forgetful. He forgets how many wheelbarrows he already has, so he buys another one, then he leaves it around the village or by the beach, but then he forgets where he's left it, so he buys another one …'

She chuckled.

'Willy and his wonderful world of wheel-barrows! I'll push it back to him tomorrow,' she said. 'I promised to dust his collection of seaweed for him anyway. It's a tricky job and he struggles with the bladderwrack.'

Slowly, slowly Danny breathed out. *She doesn't know. She hasn't seen. The dodo is safe …*

Chapter 11

FUN?

Next morning, Danny snuck downstairs early, gathered up some food and ran to the outbuilding.

'Good morning, Mr Dodo,' said Danny. 'You look well this morning. How's your foot? Bandage still on – nice one.'

The dodo clacked his beak impatiently.

'I trust you passed a pleasant night in your five-star accommodation,' he went on. 'And for today's breakfast, can I interest sir in some lightly buttered digestive biscuits (sorry, we've run out of bread), followed by cold custard with a sprinkling of Rice Krispies? Moving on, we have a side order of last night's mash with a taramasalata garnish and a handful of Hula Hoops, all washed down with fresh Highland spring water!'

Danny laid the food out on the dodo's tray as he spoke, and the bird clacked his beak excitedly before gobbling it all up.

'Oh I forgot,' he said. 'I brought crackers too.'

He threw one at the dodo, but rather than eat it, like he had that first time on the island, the dodo threw the cracker back to Danny with a neat toss of his head.

Danny laughed, and threw it back. Again, the dodo caught it. Again, he lobbed it back, like a crackery Frisbee. On and on. Until the dodo suddenly crunched up the cracker and ate it. Game over.

Then something caught Danny's eye.

'Is that a slug?' he said, curling his lip and pointing into the dodo's cubbyhole. He leaned closer. It was certainly slug shaped. But bigger. And sort of whitey grey.

'Oh no,' said Danny. 'Dodo poo! Gross!'

Slowly it dawned on him that he'd have to pick it up, like dog owners did. With a bag maybe? Or a cloth? Or a shovel? How do you clean up after a pooping dodo anyway? Probably no one in the history of the world has ever had to do that …

He ushered the dodo out of his cubby. He waddled out and watched as Danny grabbed a newspaper from a big pile nearby. He then found some old, muddy gardening gloves and put them on. Now he tried to scoop up the dodo mess, all the while pulling a face of extreme horror and turning his head away, to avoid seeing the nasty stuff, so he couldn't really see what he was doing!

'I bet Zac Hanaway didn't have to clean up after Zena the hawk,' Danny muttered as he stumbled towards the doors. 'I bet she didn't poop all over Zac's spaceship.'

Eventually, he had a big crumpled pile of newspaper, with the offending item stuck inside. He ran and dumped it in the bin outside.

'What have you got there?'

It was Granny Flora, gripping the wheelbarrow's handles, ready to push it back to Willy McNeish's.

'Oh hi, Granny,' said Danny. 'I was reading the papers, but I've finished now, so in the bin they go!'

'Right, well, nice to see you being tidy,' she said. 'See you in a few hours!'

Danny watched his granny pushing the old wheelbarrow away and then returned to the outbuilding. He slumped down on the wonky armchair, staring into space. First aid and mucking out. So far life with the dodo was less of an adventure, more like a full-time and not particularly nice job. The dodo was like a really rubbish pet, who isn't even house-trained.

'We need to get some fun on the go!' said Danny, looking at the dodo. He blinked back at him. 'It's been all bandages and poop and lying to cover up for you. We need adventure! Come on, I'm taking you out. We'll have to be careful no one sees you. Where can we go? I know! The light-house, we'll take a little stroll to the lighthouse. Did you know Granny Flora broke in there once and lit its oil lamp with her brother?'

The dodo didn't nod, but he did look a bit excited. He clacked his beak. He hopped on his good foot.

'You can't walk very well with your foot wrapped up, and the wheelbarrow's gone, but I have the solution,' said Danny. 'Pram power!'

He wheeled the old pram round to the dodo and, by getting the heavy bird to climb up on to the armchair and then giving him a bit of a shove, he got the dodo into the pram.

The pram bounced and swayed a bit with the weight of the dodo. As Danny turned it round and made for the door, the wheels squeaked noisily and the dodo bobbed about inside. Pushing slowly, they made it out into the farmyard, where it had started to drizzle.

'This is the barn,' said Danny as he wheeled the dodo towards it. 'Used to have animals or hay in there, but now it's just pretty empty.'

SQUEAK, SQUEAK – he wheeled the bouncy old pram on.

'Chicken coop,' said Danny, pointing out where the chickens lived, their big run protected by a wire-mesh fence and roof.

At the sight of the chickens pecking in the run, the dodo became excited. He started clacking his beak and flapping his stubby wings.

'Wait, hang on,' said Danny. 'What are you doing? Calm down.'

Quickly, he trotted away from the coop. The pram bounced even more, the dodo bounced inside it, the wheels splashed through puddles, the squeaking got faster and louder, then **THUMP!**

Danny pushed the pram straight into a rock on the path. On impact, the dodo pinged out of the pram, somersaulted through the air once, twice and landed in the mud by the duck pond.

'Oh help, are you OK?' Danny asked, rushing over. The dodo picked himself up and shook, like a dog who's been in the river. Thick splats of mud sprayed off him.

'You're filthy! And your bandage is coming loose. After all that effort getting it on. Never mind, it's fine, it's OK, we can sort this, we can ... Wait! Where are you going?'

The dodo had seen some ducks on the pond and was heading for the water. The ducks began flapping their wings and quacking excitedly.

'No you don't!' said Danny. 'You'll just get filthier in there.'

He tried to shoo the dodo towards the farmyard, but about eight ducks had got out of the pond now and were clucking and waddling about around the dodo, like teenagers trying to get a selfie with their favourite pop star. The dodo was strutting around too, looking really pleased with himself.

'All right, ducks, in the pond, now!' said Danny, shooing them towards the water.

'You, back in the outbuilding, now. Leave your fans and let's get you cleaned up.'

There was no way Danny could lift the dodo into the pram, so he shooed him back along the path, while the ducks stood at the edge of the pond, watching sadly as the dodo went. The dodo limped along, a length of loose bandage trailing along behind. He tried to veer off towards the chickens again when he saw them, but Danny quickly steered him, flapping and hopping towards the outbuilding.

'Now stand there while I get some water,' he said. 'Sit! OK, maybe not. Wait! Wait. Good dodo!'

He began filling a bucket from the water butt by the outbuilding doors. When he looked round the dodo had wandered off towards the barn.

'Get back here!' he hissed. 'Oh for peanuts'

sake. Here, boy! Come! You need a lead or something, I need to tie you up like a dog outside the supermarket.'

Danny ran inside and found an old tartan scarf hanging on a peg behind the coats. He gently looped it around the dodo's neck and led him back to the bucket. Danny used a flowerpot to scoop some water up and tipped it down the bird's back. The dodo squawked and shook. Too cold, maybe? Danny tried another scoop of water, but the dodo dodged out of the way. Hopeless!

Then he spotted the hose.

'Right,' he said. 'You can have a shower instead of a bath.'

He turned the hose on, but no water came out. So he turned the tap a bit more. Suddenly, a great jet of water shot out and the hose began twisting like a snake at a disco.

The dodo squawked and, with his good foot, stamped on it. The water sprayed up in the dodo's face and he leaped backwards. The hose twisted and drenched Danny's trousers, twisted again and sprayed the outbuilding doors, twisted again and again, water flying everywhere. Danny waved his hands in front of his face, trying to shield himself from the spurting water, when suddenly, the dodo pounced, grabbed the end with his beak and shook it, soaking himself, soaking Danny, and splashing the walls of the house.

Danny stumbled over to the tap and turned it off hard. Suddenly, the hose went limp in the dodo's beak.

'Phew!' said Danny. 'At least you're clean! The mud's off, but I'm soaked. Get back inside, then I can go and get dried off.'

With the dodo safely back in the

outbuilding, Danny squelched inside to change. He paused on the threshold of the kitchen, and gasped. Water was dripping off the worktop, off the table, off the walls and pooling on the floor. Then he saw the open window. The dodo had sprayed water straight through it!

Danny made a sound in his throat that sounded like a sob mixed with a growl, raced up and changed, then returned to the watery kitchen. It was as if the storm that Moira was always forecasting had hit, only inside the house, not outside.

Twelve tea towels, three bath towels, a mop, four sponges and three rolls of kitchen paper later, Danny had dried the kitchen out.

Exhausted, he pegged the towels out on the line, and was just hanging up the newspaper too, with its soaked crossword, when Granny Flora strolled back into the yard.

'Danny?' she said.

He gulped and smiled weakly.

'Er ... I just, umm, I just thought I'd do some cleaning,' he said.

Chapter 12

SQUAWK!

'Squawk!'

Danny sat up in bed. The sound had cut through his sleep, like a knife through custard.

'Squawk!
          Squawk!'

It was loud, piercing and coming from the outbuilding. Like a hideous, alternative dawn chorus, the dodo was awake and shouting his head off.

Danny raced downstairs in his pyjamas and over the gravel outside in his bare feet, wincing and hopping, before yanking open the outbuilding doors.

'Hey!' he said, running towards the cubby-hole and waving his hands. 'Quiet! Less of that, or Granny will hear.'

'Squawk!'

'Stop it!' Danny hissed, glancing over his shoulder. 'Seriously, shut up! You are not here, remember? Stop the squawking, unless you want the whole of Kinoussie to hear!'

The dodo clacked his beak impatiently at Danny.

'I won't bring you any more taramasalata if you keep this up!' Danny added.

The dodo spun around three times on the spot, then clacked his beak again.

'It's really early and you're really loud, so please, button it!' he said. 'I'm going back in to get dressed, then I'll bring you some breakfast.'

The dodo stamped impatiently.

Danny was on his way to his room when his granny called from her bedroom.

'What was that noise, Danny?'

Oh parsnips, she heard the squawking. Think quick, think quick …

'What noise?' he asked, popping his head around the door. She was sitting up in bed, looking out of the window, scanning the sky like Moira Storm. Danny noticed that there were still two pencils poking out of her hair.

'I heard a loud squawk,' she said.

'Probably just your hearing aid playing up again, Granny. Interference from the radio.

You're picking up Radio Highlands on it, maybe,' he said. 'You shouldn't wear it in bed anyway. Take it out and go back to sleep ...'

Back in his room, Danny could clearly hear the dodo squawking again. This was not good! That squawk was loud. That squawk was really squawky. That squawk was not like the sound any average garden bird would make. He looked out of his window, staring down at the roof of the outbuilding, willing the bird to stay quiet. Then he glanced at the sky and noticed a grey cloud moving towards the house. It swept and shimmered, rising and falling, swooping nearer. It wasn't a cloud, it was ...

'Pigeons?' Danny said.

A huge flock was swooping around the farmyard, like a plague of giant grey midges. Then the birds landed on the roof of the outbuilding. They began a chorus of soft

116

cooing. The sound reminded Danny of home. There were heaps of pigeons in the town where he lived. Finally, the dodo's terrible squawking stopped and, lulled by the cooing of two hundred pigeons, Danny forgot about getting the bird his breakfast and drifted off to sleep again.

He was woken for the second time that morning by the phone. It was 8.30 a.m.

'Hello?' said Danny.

'It's me,' said the voice. 'Susie. We're in trouble. We forgot to take Murdo's boat back. It's still at Clootie Bay. He's cross. You have to help me carry it back. Meet you there in half an hour.'

It took some huffing and puffing to get the boat back to Murdo's. Susie had to keep putting it down to push her glasses back up her nose and, once again, Danny was carrying it 'wrong' and creating drag. But they managed, eventually, and once the boat had been delivered, Susie and Danny plodded back towards the village, through the fine drizzle.

'What have you been up to?' Danny asked.

'Not a lot,' said Susie. 'Reading.'

'Are you cross with me?' he asked.

Susie said nothing.

'Because I brought the dodo back from the island?'

'It's not a dodo, Danny!' she said, eyes flashing behind her round glasses. 'How can it be?'

'It looks like a dodo though, doesn't it?' he said.

'Yes, it looks a bit like a dodo,' said Susie, exasperated.

'Well, that's good enough for me!' said Danny.

The two children trudged on in silence for a

while, then a bicycle bell sounded behind them. Moira Storm, bent over the handlebars as she pedalled, wobbled slowly alongside them.

'Hurry home now, children,' she warned, 'there's a storm coming!'

'But it's only drizzling a bit, Moira!' Danny said. 'It's OK.'

'FOR NOW!' Moira thundered, before wobbling off around the corner.

'Of course, technically speaking, she's right,' said Susie. 'There is always a storm coming and Moira never says when, so, she's accurate in one sense. What are you doing?'

Danny had bent over and was staring at Susie from under his blond fringe. He jabbed his finger at her.

'Susie, away off home now!' he said, in his best Scottish accent. 'There's a storm heading this way. A terrible storm with thunder to split your head in two!'

Susie looked away, trying to hide her smile.

'Auch, you think it's only drizzle, you think it's all right, you think all's well with the world,' Danny continued, then he hobbled up to Susie and jabbed her in the ribs. 'Maybe! Maybe it is! FOR NOW!'

Susie batted his finger away, but he kept poking her and roaring 'FOR NOW!' until she was giggling and wriggling and laughing. Then Danny stood up to his full height, laughing too.

'Come on,' he said, when the laughter had died down. 'Come with me to see the dodo. I bandaged up his foot and I'm feeding him lots. He's quite, erm, lively though. Just needs a bit of training!'

Susie chewed her lip, unsure.

'You don't have to say it's a dodo or believe in it or anything,' Danny added. 'It's just something to do, isn't it? If I had a dog or a cat, you might come to see it, right? Well, it's kind of the same, but different. What do you reckon?'

Susie looked at Danny, then gave a tiny nod; a nod just big enough to make her super-straight fringe twitch.

'OK, I'll come,' she said. 'But I'm not using the d-word!'

'What, Danny?'

'No!' sighed Susie. 'Dodo!'

'Whoops, you just did!'

'Arrgghh!' said Susie. 'That was the last time. Never again. Got it?'

'No d-word,' said Danny. 'Got it!'

Chapter 13

VISIT

'What are all these pigeons doing here?' Susie asked, when they arrived in the farmyard. The pigeons were perched along the roof of the outbuilding again. Danny shrugged.

'We don't usually have pigeons here,' Susie insisted. 'Not in these numbers. This isn't Trafalgar Square, you know.'

At the sound of the outbuilding doors being pushed open, the dodo began to clack his beak. Danny shushed him as he hopped across the junk towards the corner cubbyhole.

'I've brought a friend!' he said. 'Remember Susie?'

'Hello,' she said. 'Oh, I can't believe I just did that. It's not like it's going to answer back!'

The dodo stared at her. Susie noticed how the bird seemed quite different to the creature they had brought back from the island; stronger looking, with brighter eyes.

'See how well he looks!' said Danny, proudly. 'Remember how skinny he was on the island? Look at him now! I've been feeding him taramasalata, and other stuff too, like Hula Hoops and custard creams.'

'Are you sure that's a good diet for a bird?' Susie asked. 'Wouldn't it prefer …'

'It's fine! He loves the same food as me,' said Danny.

'Yes, but I'm sure I've read that this kind of large bird, not using the d-word, would need fresh food, such as …'

'SQUAWK!'

The two children jumped.

'Well, that's loud!' said Susie.

'SQUAWK!'

'Shush, please, Dodo, keep the noise down!' Danny said.

'SQUAWK!'

'I don't know why he's started squawking like this,' said Danny. 'He's a bit of a handful. Not quite how I imagined he might be.'

'How did you imagine he'd be?'

'I dunno,' said Danny. 'Like a dog, but way better, you know? More like a sidekick dog. A pet, but a really extra cool one!'

'A pet?' Susie said. 'It's not a pet. It's wild!'

'SQUAWK!' said the dodo.

'He is pretty wild, but we have to shut him up, or we'll have the whole of Kinoussie here!' said Danny.

'More than Kinoussie,' said Susie. 'If the villagers were stupid enough to think like you think, that this is a you-know-what, word would spread around the country, around the world!'

Danny gulped.

'Scientists, naturalists, they would all want to find out more about him, take him away, maybe run tests and experiments,' said Susie. 'Plus, the media would be up here, swarming all over the village. Any local that wanted to make money could just sell a few photos or their own story. Simple!'

Then Susie pushed her glasses up her nose and smiled.

'Luckily though, this is, quite obviously, not an extinct bird,' she said. 'It's not a you-know-what. So I wouldn't worry too much about it being discovered.'

'SQUAWK!'

'Shush, please, double please with extra sauce!' said Danny, thinking about all those scientists who would rush up to Kinoussie and seize the dodo the second they found out about him. That must not happen! But what if Granny Flora heard him, or Moira Storm? They might spread the word. There were no secrets in Kinoussie, after all! And what about Wee Jimmie? Danny remembered him talking about searching the outbuilding for treasure and doing a deal with people back in Glasgow. He didn't trust Wee Jimmie. He felt sure that if Wee Jimmie found out, he'd spy his chance to make some money. He wouldn't hesitate to grab the dodo and take him away.

'Squawk!' went the dodo again.

Susie covered her ears. 'I thought you said everything was going well,' she said.

'It was!' said Danny. 'Maybe he doesn't like you.'

'Oh no you don't,' said Susie. 'You don't get to blame me, Danny. Not for any of this. I said all along you should leave that bird where you found it.'

'OK, OK, sorry,' said Danny. 'It's just this morning that he's started squawking. But he can't be found! That would be terrible.'

Danny thought briefly about Fat Hamaway, his hamster. He had let him out and he'd escaped under the floorboards and was lost. Danny couldn't lose another pet like that. He had to do it right this time.

A scratching sound above made the children look up. There, in the corner of the outbuilding, perched on a beam, was a pigeon. It had squeezed its way in through a gap between the wall and the roof. Then another appeared, and another, and another. They all shimmied up, until a line of about thirty pigeons had assembled just above the dodo's cubbyhole. They began cooing excitedly and bobbing their heads. The dodo replied, like he was greeting his long-lost friends, clacking his beak and making a cute cooing sound back;

127

a sound that Danny had never heard before. But then the pigeons suddenly noticed Susie and Danny. They cocked their heads and stared.

'Why are they staring at us?' Danny asked, nervously.

Then, as if following some secret signal, they all flew off their perch at once.

'They're heading straight for us,' shrieked Susie.

'Run!' yelled Danny.

The two children fled for the doors as the

pigeons wheeled above and then dive-bombed them, pecking their clothes and hair. Danny grabbed the dodo's metal food tray and tried to use it as a shield. Pigeon beaks tapped against it like bullets. Susie flung the doors open and raced out. Danny followed and they slammed them shut, panting. The doors rattled as a few pigeons flew against them, then everything went quiet.

Danny knelt down and peeped through a hole low down in the door.

'What are they doing?' whispered Susie.

'They're back by the dodo again,' said Danny.

'Let me see.' She shoved Danny aside, crouched down and peered in. 'Dropping things out of their beaks! Look!'

He peered in. 'They're sort of coughing up stuff. Are they being sick?'

'Let me see,' said Susie, looking in. 'They're not being sick, they're dropping seeds and berries, I think. The dodo's eating it all up. Wait, of course, they're *feeding* it!'

Susie kept talking, her eye peering through the tiny hole in the doors.

'How fascinating. This is extraordinary. They're bringing it food. Of course! This must be how the dodo survived on the island. The pigeons flew over with scraps of food. Incredible!'

'Why would they do that?' Danny asked.

'Well, I'm pretty sure pigeons and dodos were related. So it's one family helping another family member.'

Danny grinned.

'So you admit it's a dodo?' he said.

'What?'

'You just said dodos are related to pigeons, which suggests you think this is a dodo, as those birds in there are, most certainly, pigeons.'

Susie pointed her finger at Danny.

'And *you* just said I wouldn't have to admit it was a dodo, or believe in it,' she said. 'Just now, before we got here.'

'Fine, but *you* used the d-word, not me!' said Danny, still grinning. 'Just saying!'

Back at the house, Granny Flora was getting ready to go out.

'Did I just hear squawking again?' she said, when the two children appeared in the kitchen.

Danny felt his cheeks burn pink again.

'That was my eagle impression,' he said quickly. 'Pretty good, isn't it?'

'I suppose,' said Granny Flora. 'Bit squawky for an eagle though, don't you think, Roddy? They do more of a ka-kaarrr sound!'

'Aye,' said Roddy, thoughtfully.

'Anyway, it's time we left, Roddy. We're off

to Fort Plother to do some shopping. You've been eating us out of house and home so far. Getting through crackers and digestive biscuits like there's no tomorrow. But I suppose you are a growing boy. You two be good, help yourself to lunch in the larder – there's still a little bit of food in there! I'll be back in about two hours.'

The children grabbed some biscuits and headed up to Danny's room.

'I don't get why the dodo has started squawking like this,' he said.

Susie barely heard him. She was writing in a notebook.

'This is a truly fascinating example of interspecies dependency,' she said, scribbling.

'I'm sure it's nothing. He's just having an off day. We all have off days,' said Danny, munching thoughtfully on a third custard cream.

'It's extremely rare to see this level of cooperation between two loosely related species in the wild,' Susie went on.

'Perhaps I should get him some toys? Do they have any pet toys in the Spar in the village? Or maybe a football? I could rig up a little goal for him,' Danny said.

Susie continued making notes and Danny lay there, lost in thought for a long while, until the sounds of scuffling and lots of small wings beating drifted in from outside. Danny knelt on his bed and looked out of the window. The pigeons were assembling on the roof of the outbuilding again. They were hopping about and ruffling their wings. They seemed excited, like a crowd waiting for a match to start.

'What are they up to?' Danny muttered.

'... sharing food is another unusual beha-viour generally only seen between single

133

species …' Susie murmured, scribbling furiously.

'Something's up,' Danny said, and then he heard it. **Thump!** And again. **Thump!** He scrambled off his bed, sprinted downstairs and ran out into the yard, just in time to hear one last thump before the outbuilding doors flew open and the dodo, running at high speed, raced out.

Chapter 14

OUT

The dodo ran. He ran fast. Who knew dodos could run so fast?

'It's heading for the chicken coop!' said Susie, who had just arrived in the yard. 'What do we do?'

'After him!' said Danny.

As the children got nearer they could hear the sound of excited squawking from the dodo, and upset clucking from the chickens.

'Oh my flip!' panted Danny. 'He's broken in.'

The gate to the chicken coop was open and the dodo was inside, chasing the chickens, his beak open with excitement. Upset hens kept running and fluttering out of the way, dodging the giant bird. Susie tried to stop them escaping through the broken gate, while Danny attempted to shoo the dodo out. No good. The hens were off and the dodo, with no more birds to chase, had run into the henhouse.

Danny peeped in and then stumbled backwards into Susie.

'What?' she said. 'You've gone white.'

'He's a cannibal!' said Danny, pointing at the henhouse.

Susie looked in. Oh dear. The dodo was having eggs for lunch. He was moving from nest box to nest box, cracking the shells of each egg with the tip of his huge beak and slurping up the runny insides. It was egg carnage.

'Another fascinating insight into the bird's diet, Danny, and that's a great protein supply right there which will really boost his strength,' Susie said, and was about to

reach for her notebook, when she saw his look of panic and horror. 'I'll jot that down later ...'

'We have to get him out of there and back in the outbuilding before Granny gets home,' said Danny, breathless, but when he tried to shoo him out the dodo jabbed his beak at him. It was like trying to take a sausage off a hungry dog.

Danny waited, hopelessly, until the dodo had eaten every last egg. The bird then waddled out of the henhouse, stood on the grass and did an enormous burp. Danny and Susie grimaced. Bloated with eggs, the dodo now seemed calm. Talking to him quietly and moving slowly, Danny coaxed him out of the coop.

'Susie, try to catch the hens, while I get him locked back in the outbuilding,' he said over his shoulder as he ushered the dodo back through the farmyard.

Susie ran off in search of the stray hens, lunging at them as they darted about.

Who knew chickens could run so fast?

Moving cautiously, keeping an eye out for his granny, Danny finally got the dodo back inside the outbuilding. He sighed deeply.

'I can't catch them!' puffed Susie, running up to Danny as he secured the doors. 'They won't stand still. It's really annoying!'

'We'll have to tell Granny Flora,' said Danny, looking stricken. 'The hens escaped, the eggs are all smashed and the coop gate is off its hinges.'

'What will you say?' Susie asked. 'An extinct bird with an attitude problem did it?'

'I don't know,' said Danny, and he started spinning slowly around on the spot.

'What are you doing?' Susie asked.

'It's what the dodo does when he's stressed,' said Danny.

'Is it helping?'

'Not sure. Don't think so.' He stopped and stood there, swaying a bit.

'Dizzy?' Susie asked.

'Yes,' said Danny. 'I know, I'll just say it was a fox that got into the coop. I hate lying, but what else can I do?'

'Tell her the truth?' Susie suggested. 'Surely she can keep it to herself?'

'Are you kidding?' said Danny. 'There are no secrets in Kinoussie! She'd say something and Wee Jimmie would hear, and then it's all over! They would take the dodo off me or Wee Jimmie would sell him. They'd do weird science tests on him and scare him and they don't know that he likes taramasalata on mash or how he likes to play with washers on a string or ...'

Granny Flora's car pulled into the farmyard.

'It was a fox, OK?' Danny whispered as his granny got out of her car and came to greet them.

'Hello, kids!' Granny Flora said. 'What have you two been up to? More fun in the outbuilding?'

Danny gulped.

'Well, actually, not really, because ...' said Susie.

'It was a fox!' blurted Danny. 'I mean, *there* was a fox. It got into the chicken coop and ate all the eggs.'

'Did you see it?' Granny Flora asked, frowning.

'Not exactly, no,' said Danny. 'But we found all the broken eggs.'

Granny Flora dropped her handbag and ran off towards the coop.

Who knew grannies could run so fast?

The children followed.

'Very strange,' she said, after inspecting the damage. 'Foxes tend to come out at night, and they usually dig under the fence, they don't break the gate. Did it take any of the hens?'

'No,' said Danny. 'They just escaped through the open gate. We tried to catch them, but they're too fast.'

'Well, perhaps at dusk they'll naturally come home to roost,' said Granny, looking around to see where the hens had strayed. 'But I'll need to get the coop fixed before then. I'm calling Wee Jimmie.'

Wee Jimmie had the chicken coop repaired by teatime, but just like Granny Flora, he was not convinced by Danny and Susie's explanation.

'Why would a fox be out in broad daylight?' Wee Jimmie asked, to no one in particular, as he swigged the tea Granny had made for him (strong, plenty of milk, five sugars). He was leaning against his van in the farmyard, wearing his red woolly hat, which looked like an angry mosquito bite on his head. Shirley the chihuahua was yapping inside. Danny offered Wee Jimmie a biscuit, which he crammed into his mouth in one.

'Who ever heard of a fox eating eggs over chickens?' said Wee Jimmie. 'It would be like me choosing salad in a steakhouse! Never going to happen!'

Danny laughed nervously, offering up a silent prayer that his bird wouldn't start thumping at the doors or squawking while they were all stood outside. Luckily, the last time Danny checked, just before Wee Jimmie arrived, the dodo was in an eggy-induced sleep, like a great-uncle conked out in the corner after Christmas lunch.

'Well, that coop is secure,' said Wee Jimmie. 'A rhino couldn't get in there now.'

'I just have to hope the chickens make their way back before nightfall,' said Granny Flora. 'They do like to snuggle down in their boxes at night, and they have a kind of homing instinct.'

'Bit like them,' said Wee Jimmie, raising his eyebrows. 'Are they bothering you?'

'What? The children?' said Granny Flora.

'No, the pigeons,' said Wee Jimmie, pointing at the outbuilding roof. Everyone looked up. A huge flock had settled there again and the birds were fidgeting about, cooing and pooping white splashes down the tiles.

'I've never seen so many pigeons up here in Kinoussie,' said Wee Jimmie. 'We had lots down in Glasgow, of course, but not up here. What do they want with your outbuilding?'

'Danny's been feeding them!' Susie spluttered.

Danny glanced quickly at her. Was this a genius lie or a disastrous blurt?

'Like you do in Trafalgar Square, in London, you know?' she went on. 'It's because he's from the South. That's what they do down there.'

'Well, you should stop that, before they damage your gran's roof,' said Wee Jimmie, thrusting his empty tea mug at Danny. 'Flora, if you want me to fix spikes to the top, to keep them off, I can. I'd need to go inside too, to check if they can get in. You don't want three hundred pigeons roosting inside your outbuilding, do you?'

'Most certainly not,' said Granny Flora. 'They'd make a mess and a racket. It's bad

145

enough all that squawking I've been hearing.'

'**Atishoo!**' went Danny, flinging the mug up in the air. It smashed on the gravel behind him. He was desperate to cause a distraction from the conversation about loud, unusual squawking coming from the outbuilding.

Wee Jimmie gave him his small-eyed stare. The one Danny hated; the one that made him think Wee Jimmie was capable of doing very bad things indeed.

'Oh Danny, that was one of my favourite mugs! Moira gave it to me for finding her false teeth on the beach two summers ago. Never mind. Are you getting a cold? Let's get you in before you catch a chill. You're not used to Scottish summer weather,' said Granny Flora, putting an arm around him and heading for the house.

'Remember about the spikes,' said Wee Jimmie.

On the doorstep, Danny glanced back. Wee Jimmie was still staring at him, his eyes narrowed to suspicious little slits. Then he climbed into his van and drove out of the farmyard, Shirley yapping from the dashboard.

Chapter 15

TORN

Danny slept fitfully that night. He had bad dream after bad dream. He dreamed he was running down a corridor that kept getting longer. Then he dreamed that Fat Hamaway came back after years under the floorboards and was the size of a hippo with giant beaver teeth. And then, worst of all, he dreamed that the dodo flew out of his granny's outbuilding and went on the rampage, eating chickens, snatching Roddy Aye's knitting needles, and shredding Wee Jimmie's red woolly hat with his bare claws ...

Sadly, waking up didn't offer much relief from the nightmares.

'Squawk!'

The dodo! It was like yesterday morning

repeating itself all over again. Luckily, Granny Flora now slept without her hearing aid, but even so, this racket had to stop.

Danny ran across the farmyard and opened the outbuilding doors. He paused for a second, blinking and rubbing his eyes. Had it snowed? Inside? The outbuilding was covered in white: mountains of white! He stepped cautiously in. The white mounds crumpled and rustled under his feet. Not snow, but newspaper! A blizzard of shredded newspaper, all over the outbuilding!

'What have you been *doing*?' Danny hissed.

He couldn't see the dodo, but he could see what he had done. He'd knocked over a huge tower of old newspapers and ripped them to ribbons!

'You've shredded the lot!' said Danny. 'How am I going to clear this up?'

He waded through drifts of newspaper

until he was standing by the cubby. It was full to the top with shredded paper. Danny couldn't see the dodo but he could hear him rustling inside. Suddenly, the dodo's head popped out. He was holding a single sheet of newspaper in his beak.

'What's that?' Danny asked. 'Can I see?'

The dodo pulled his head back a bit.

'I want to see what you're holding,' Danny said. 'You've shredded everything else, but not that one page. What is it?'

He reached his hand out slowly, but the dodo flapped his stubby wings angrily, sending a storm of shredded paper up into the air and across the floor. Danny leaped back and fell into the lopsided armchair.

'OK, I get it!' he said. 'That piece of news-paper is really important to you!'

Most of the paper had blown away now and he could see the dodo clearly. He stared defiantly at Danny for a second then dropped the newspaper and stood on it firmly.

Danny eased himself off the chair and, reaching out his hand, began to lean in towards the paper the dodo was standing on. The dodo squawked, then yanked at the string of washers Danny had hung from the bamboo cane above the cubbyhole, snapping it. Hundreds of rusty washers tumbled to the

ground. The dodo picked one up and flung it at Danny. This was like cracker Frisbee, but this time played with small metal rings.

'Hey!' Danny yelled. 'Stop it!'

Ping! Another washer ricocheted off the wall. **Thud, thud, thud,** three more peppered Danny's chest. He was under attack from tiny hurled washers, spun at him from the beak of an extinct bird. At 5.15 in the morning! You really couldn't make it up.

'Stop it! Stop it! Stop it already!' said Danny, batting the washers away like they were a swarm of angry wasps. He grabbed the dodo's metal food tray from the ground and used it as a shield. Washers pinged off it like bullets off a speeding getaway car.

'STOP IT!' Danny yelled. 'Or no more taramasalata! DO I MAKE MYSELF CLEAR?'

Silence. Then a single beak clack.

'I am going to drop my shield now,' said Danny, still crouched behind it. 'You chuck one more washer and that's it. The fish dip stops.'

Another clack of irritation from the bird.

He lowered the tray. The dodo stared at him, a fierce look in his eyes. Danny didn't like that look.

The newspaper page was still pinned beneath the dodo's foot. Danny looked down at it. He could just make out that it was a travel article, showing a photo of a white sandy beach with palm trees and lush jungle. Where was that place? Why did it matter to the bird?

'I give up,' he said, a little huffily. 'I'm going back to bed. You can keep your precious newspaper, whatever it is.'

As Danny pushed the outbuilding doors closed he noticed that the pigeons had arrived on the roof of the outbuilding.

'Oh no …! Not them again,' he muttered.

The pigeons heard him. They took off in one fluttery, feathery grey cloud. Danny dropped the rope that tied the outbuilding door shut and began running for the front door. The pigeons swooped once over the farmyard, then flew very low and very fast, directly at Danny.

He dived on to the ground, just in time. The pigeons swooped over him once, then rose up, turned and swooped again. He could feel the air ruffling his hair as they flew past. He reached for a bucket by the water butt and put it over his head as a defence. But then he heard it. A squawk. *That* squawk! The one he had come to know so well. Danny peeped out from under his bucket and saw the dodo standing outside the outbuilding, sniffing the early morning air, looking – he had to admit it – absolutely majestic. The drizzle settled on his grey feathers like tiny diamonds. The tip of his beak looked like it had been dipped in liquid gold, his leathery grey face looked ... Actually, that still looked grey and leathery.

The pigeons were thrilled and excited to see their dodo friend and began flying in a tight circle above him. Then, with a beat of his short wings and a triumphant squawk, the dodo raced away.

Chapter 16

GOOSEBERRIES

'He's heading for the chicken coop again,' gasped Danny, staring after the dodo as it bounded off. 'Hang on, no, he's not. He's stopped.'

He watched as the bird paused, sniffed and trotted off to the right. He was heading for Granny Flora's fruit bushes. Danny was a fast runner, but by the time he got there, the dodo had already stripped one bush of all its gooseberries. The gooseberries were sharp and acidic, the bush covered with pointy thorns, but the dodo wasn't put off. He ripped huge beakfuls of berries at a time, swallowing them whole, like a pelican gobbling up snooker balls.

'No, no, no!' said Danny. 'Stop. I can bring

you breakfast. You don't need to do this! Those are not your berries! They're Granny's. She was planning to make a fool out of them.'

Instead, the dodo was making a fool out of Danny.

He hopped pathetically, unable to make the dodo stop feasting.

Finally, when the dodo had finished eating, Danny was able to shoo him back towards the outbuilding. Just like after his egg binge, he seemed happy to come, walking slowly, clearly full after his all-you-can-eat breakfast. Boy and bird were just steps away from the outbuilding, its doors still open, when the dodo stopped again.

'Oh please, what now?' Danny muttered. 'Look! You have to go back inside, right now, before my granny gets up and sees you. Please!'

The urge to do a stress spin on the spot

was great, but Danny didn't dare take his eyes off the bird. The dodo, on the other hand, was looking at his feet; or, at what his feet stood on. Gravel. He lowered his head, scooped up a few of the tiny stones and swallowed them down.

'Oh my ... WHAT?' said Danny. 'You're eating gravel. *Gravel!* Why? You're going to die or be sick or ... Stop it! Stop it!'

The bird bent and scooped up a few more stones, knocking them back in one big swallow. Danny jumped about in front of the bird, waving his hands, trying to stop him from gobbling up more stones. Then the dodo began to beat his wings.

'Why are you flapping?' he said. 'Are you choking? Oh flip ... Hold on.'

Danny leaped on to the dodo, his long legs straddling his back, keeping the wings pressed firmly to the bird's sides. Then Danny linked his hands under the plump body and, with a sharp punch, he pulled them in against the dodo's chest, making him squawk, retch and spray out a scattering of stones.

'That's the way!' said Danny, regaining his balance as the dodo shifted beneath him. 'Don't panic. It's just the Heimlich manoeuvre!

I'm saving you. You are probably the very last dodo alive today. I won't let anything hurt you. Not on my watch, Dodo, not on my watch!'

Danny yanked his arms in hard again, but this time he lost his balance. Danny and the dodo somersaulted backwards in a roly-poly of boy and bird, grey feathers, blue jeans and yellow, clawed feet.

Danny felt dizzy. He sneezed on some of the dodo's downy feathers, and then sat up, a shower of gravel tumbling from his clothes, frantically looking around.

'Dodo?' said Danny. 'Dodo?'

But the dodo was gone, a grey speck racing in the direction of Clootie Bay.

Chapter 17

LIES

'Are you OK, Danny?'

It was Granny Flora. In the kerfuffle, Danny hadn't heard her leave the house. Now she was standing over him, holding a large bowl. Oh flip! Had she seen the dodo running off? Had she watched them rolling around on the ground?

'Up you get now. You look like you've seen a ghost,' she said, patting his pale cheek.

Er, not a ghost, Danny thought. *Just a supposedly extinct flightless bird that refuses to do as it's told.*

But Granny seemed like Granny as usual – warm, cheerful, steady – and not at all like she'd just seen a wrestling match between a boy and a dodo.

'Come on,' she said, marching across the farmyard. 'It's gooseberry gathering day! We will be dining on fool tonight!'

Danny closed his eyes and wobbled a bit. Why now? Why did Granny Flora have to pick the gooseberries now? Couldn't he have some breakfast, a drink at least, before the next round of chaos; the next dodo disaster; the next lie?

He ran to catch up with her and laid a hand on her sleeve. 'Sorry!' he said.

'For what?' said Granny Flora.

'The gooseberries,' he said. 'I ate them all. They were so fresh and juicy. I couldn't stop.'

Granny looked baffled and cross all in one.

'But they're sour, Danny!' she said. 'How could you stand to eat them all? They're so sharp!'

'I like the taste, only perhaps now I feel a

162

bit sick,' he said, doubling over, one hand pressed to his tummy.

'Right, let's get you in,' she said. 'A bowl of soothing porridge will take the edge off all that acidic fruit.'

Oh great. Porridge. Danny's least favourite food. Thanks a bunch, Dodo, for an off-the-scale-of-terrible start to the day. As he limped miserably inside, he wondered where the dodo was now and how he would ever find him. Then, with a twinge of guilt, he wondered if he even wanted to find him again. This adventure seemed to be slipping out of his control.

After slowly working his way through a large bowl of Granny Flora's porridge, Danny rang Susie.

'Disaster!' he said. 'The dodo got out, with help from the pigeons, then he ate all the gooseberries!'

'I knew it!' said Susie.

'Knew what?'

'All that stuff you've been feeding it is wrong – I knew it! It needs fresh fruit.'

'But I hate fruit!' spluttered Danny. 'I thought me and the dodo liked the same things! Hula Hoops and custard and taramasalata!'

'You should have done your research,

Danny,' said Susie, sounding just a tiny bit smug. 'Birds like yours eat fruit, seeds and roots.'

'Roots!' exclaimed Danny. 'Why would it want to eat muddy old roots? It's not an animal!'

Susie sighed for a moment, not bothering to answer that one.

'Never mind, what happened next?' she asked.

'Well, after the gooseberries, he ate some stones, so I did the Heimlich manoeuvre on him, and then we kind of fell over and then ...'

'Wait!' said Susie. 'Slow down. First of all, there was no need to give him the Heimlich. Many birds eat small stones to help digestion. The stones sit in their gizzard and act as internal teeth. It's normal.'

'Gizzard?' Danny spluttered. He held the phone away from his face and stared at it, shaking his head in disbelief. 'You're using the word gizzard and then you're telling me eating gravel is totally fine. How was I supposed to know any of that?'

'Like I said, you could have read some books, instead of just thinking the bird will automatically like the food you like. I like haggis, so you must, right?'

'Don't get smart on me,' said Danny.

'I was born smart, Danny. I can't help it,' said Susie. 'So, what happened after the Heimlich?'

'He ran off, towards the beach,' said Danny.

'Did you go after it?'

'No, I had to come in and eat absolutely flipping loads of horrible porridge.'

'Porridge, at a time like this?' Susie shrieked. 'Danny, you need to get out there before someone sees it!'

Danny was quiet for a while.

'You said yourself you don't want anyone else getting their hands on it,' Susie added.

Danny sighed heavily.

'Don't flake out now,' said Susie sternly. 'You brought this bird home, now you have to take responsibility for it.'

'Can't you?' Danny said. It just slipped out.

'Me!' shouted Susie. 'I will help you find it, but that bird is your problem, not mine. I made that clear from the start, remember? You brought it off the island. This was the adventure you wanted!'

'But the adventure's gone all wrong! The dodo is so wild!' spluttered Danny. 'After all I've done for him too! I thought he'd be grateful!'

'I don't think birds understand that,' said Susie. 'Look, just because you're not crazy about how it's acting doesn't mean you can turn your back on it. Imagine if I gave you a puppy and ten days later you wanted to give it back because it had peed on your bedroom floor. Or because it chewed your Zac Hanaway comics. Would that be OK?'

'No, it would not be OK if it chewed my comics,' said Danny, but before Susie could erupt, he went on. 'Look, I get it! I get what you're saying. I have to take responsibility. It's my bird and I can't give up on him. I can't let him escape, like I did with Fat Hamaway.'

'Who's Fat Hamaway?'

'A hamster I had once, but I let him out and he disappeared under the floorboards.'

'Well, this is no hamster, Danny,' said Susie. 'It's a wild animal, and it really needs your help.'

Chapter 18

ESCAPE

Susie waded through the drifts of shredded newspaper in the outbuilding and found Danny curled up in the lopsided armchair, staring into the dodo's empty cubbyhole.

'What are you doing?' she said. 'Come on, let's go. We have to find your bird. What's wrong with you?'

Danny passed her the ripped newspaper page that the dodo had found and protected, the one showing a tropical beach.

'The dodo ripped it out,' he said. 'He tore up tons of newspapers but stopped when he got to this page. Then he wouldn't hand it over. He threw loads of washers at me to stop me looking, which hurt! Why?'

'Well, washers would hurt if thrown at the

right speed,' muttered Susie, studying the beach picture. Danny got up and stood next to her, squinting at it and then at the piles of newspaper around them. Suddenly, he noticed a different scrap of newspaper. He picked it up, stared at it for some time, then showed it to Susie.

'Does he look familiar?' he said, his voice oddly quiet.

There was a police photofit image of a criminal. Danny stared at the face for a while. The image was rough and basic, but there was no mistaking who it was.

'Wee Jimmie,' gasped Susie. 'What does it say?'

'It's all ripped,' said Danny, 'but here's something – "notorious criminal James Finlay … on the run after bungled burglary of the something something … dangerous … apprehended in local tattoo parlour but made his escape through …" Then it's all shredded, I can't read any more.'

Danny stared at Susie.

'I had a bad feeling about Wee Jimmie and now I know why!' he said. 'He's a wanted man. He was definitely going to have HATE tattooed on his hand. He's on the run! What should we do? Should we call the police?'

'There's only Sergeant MacDuff up here,

and he covers a massive area,' said Susie. 'Plus, it's Tuesday and he does his pottery class in Fort Plother.'

Danny thrust his fingers into his hair and spun on the spot three times.

'We have to find the dodo,' he said. 'Right now! He's out there, alone, and Wee Jimmie, a dangerous criminal, might find him!'

'Let's take this,' said Susie, grabbing an old fishing net that was hanging from the roof. 'Could come in handy!'

The children ran towards Clootie Bay and were deep in the oak and birch woods that lined the shore when they heard a crashing sound, like branches breaking. Peering through the trees they could just make out the dodo. He had stepped awkwardly on to a fallen tree trunk, edged along it and, with a violent flap of his tiny wings, jumped off. The children stood silently for several minutes, watching the dodo repeat this, over and over. Each time, the bird landed clumsily in the leaves. Throwing a frozen turkey out of a top-floor window would have looked more elegant.

'What's he doing?' Danny whispered.

'Not sure,' said Susie, 'but take the net and see if you can catch him.'

Danny tiptoed through the woods, following a wide arc around the dodo and coming up behind him. The bird had clambered back on to the tree trunk and was stretching out his wings again, preparing to jump.

Danny lifted the huge net, but just as he was about to bring it down over the dodo's head, the bird looked round.

Their eyes locked for one, two, three seconds. Danny's eyes were full of apology, the dodo's full of questions.

'Sorry!' Danny whispered, and he slammed the net down.

Instantly, the dodo began squawking and struggling inside it. His stout legs kicked and he lunged and twisted inside the trap.

'Stop, please, don't fight it,' said Danny, trying to control the net. The bird tumbled off the tree trunk, pulling Danny with him. The dodo lay on his side, one leg still kicking out, his eye lasering up at Danny from inside the net.

'I'm sorry! I'm so sorry!' said Danny. 'I just want to bring you home! Home, Dodo!'

He eased the net up slowly and the bird lay still for a second. Then he shook himself violently and stood up, holding Danny's gaze angrily, beak open. Danny didn't move. He looked sadly at the beautiful bird as it turned, squawked and hurtled off into the woods.

'Catch it, Danny!' Susie shouted. She had seen the whole thing. But Danny dropped the net, letting the dodo disappear into the trees.

'Why did you let it escape?' Susie panted, when she caught up with Danny. But he didn't speak. He was standing dead still, his shoulders stooped, his eyes on the ground.

Susie knew not to question him any further. He looked miserable. She picked up the net and the pair trudged along in silence until they were just outside the farmyard, when Danny froze. Wee Jimmie's van was parked there.

'Just stay calm and don't say anything,' said Susie. 'The dodo isn't here, after all. He's off in the woods. Wee Jimmie can't find him right now.'

Wee Jimmie was fixing spikes on to the roof of the outbuilding, to keep the pigeons off. Danny noticed, with a hiccup of his heart, that the outbuilding doors were wide open. The children walked quietly into the yard, serenaded by Shirley the chihuahua yip-yapping frantically inside the van, her bug eyes almost popping out of her head. At the noise, Wee Jimmie came down his ladder.

'Getting rid of these pigeons for your gran,' he said, looking at Danny. 'I've put spikes up and also blocked a hole, so they can't get inside any more. Looks like they were roosting right over the corner, but you'd know about that, wouldn't you, Danny? I can see you've been playing there. Ripping up newspaper like there's no tomorrow!'

Danny said nothing.

'Looks like there's some kind of nest in there too, with a blanket and water buckets and whatnot,' said Wee Jimmie. 'Been keeping something there? One of the chickens or a stray cat? Or something more

176

valuable. An eagle! Or maybe you've tracked down the last wolf in Scotland and got him tucked in there! People would pay good money to see one of them!'

Wee Jimmie chuckled darkly and scratched his head through his red woolly hat. Still Danny said nothing.

'Seriously, though, there are food crumbs on the ground and I'm worried they could attract rats,' said Wee Jimmie. 'So I'm just going to let Shirley check it out. She may be small but she has a good nose on her and she's brilliant at flushing out vermin!'

Wee Jimmie grinned and yanked open the van door. Shirley exploded out like an angry yapping guinea pig fired from a canon and began sniffing the ground feverishly.

'Looks like she's picked up a scent,' said Wee Jimmie, eyes sparkling. Danny gulped.

177

Shirley then skipped into the outbuilding and ran straight for the cubbyhole.

'She's sniffing the blanket!' Wee Jimmie said, peering in and then turning to beam at the children. 'She's on to something!'

Susie reached for Danny's hand and gripped it, but neither of them said a word. Had Shirley picked up the dodo's scent? And if she had, what would she do now?

Follow it, that's what. Shirley shot out of the outbuilding and raced off down the path to Clootie Bay.

Who knew chihuahuas could run so fast?

Wee Jimmie took off after her.

'Come on!' said Susie, pointing the net in the direction of Clootie Bay. 'Follow them. Quick!'

Chapter 19

HUNTED

Wee Jimmie had only made it a little way down the path before he had to stop, out of breath and red in the face.

Who knew Wee Jimmie could run so slowly?

Danny and Susie shot past him, trying to spot Shirley or the dodo, or both. A crashing sound over in the trees made them stop.

'There!' said Susie. 'Dodo! Straight ahead. Moving fast. But what's that on his back?'

'Shirley!' screeched Danny.

Shirley had followed the dodo's scent, found him and, somehow, climbed on to his back. The tiny dog was now riding him like a horse. It was like the maddest circus act you've never seen. And fast too.

'They're going back to the farm,' said Susie. 'Wee Jimmie will see them! He's coming down the path!'

Danny grabbed the net and took a swipe at Shirley as she galloped past, perched on the dodo's back. Missed! The dodo didn't stop and Shirley, somehow, managed to hang on. The pair was now heading towards Wee Jimmie.

Summoning all the power of his porridge breakfast, Danny ran at full speed on his long legs, passing the dodo, and sped around the corner to where Wee Jimmie was still leaning on a gate post, still panting, still red in the face.

'On your head! Don't move,' said Danny. 'A dangerous insect!'

Then he slammed the net down over Wee Jimmie's head.

The huge man struggled and wriggled, pawing at the net, but Danny held on to it, like he was taming a wild – and slightly fat – Scottish stallion.

The dodo, with Shirley on top, shot past, with Wee Jimmie still staggering about and roaring, unaware of the extinct bird and chihuahua double act that had just passed within metres of him.

'What are you doing?' he bellowed. 'Get. This. Thing. Off. Me!'

With a huge shove, Wee Jimmie heaved the net up and off, then ripped it out of Danny's shaking hands and flung it into the trees.

'What's your game, sonny?' he asked, the hand that almost said HATE scrunched into a meaty fist. Danny's terrified eyes flickered over towards the farmyard in the distance, then back to Wee Jimmie's face – a tiny move-ment, but the big man spotted it.

Wee Jimmie turned, just as the dodo sped into the outbuilding.

'What was that?' he said. 'Going in there? I saw something! Running into the outbuilding. You're hiding something. What is it?'

'It's nothing. You saw nothing!' said Danny, but Wee Jimmie turned and began jogging back to the farmyard.

Danny didn't dare run ahead. He couldn't. All the energy seemed to have drained out of him. He felt as limp as six-week-old salad. Nothing could save the dodo now. It was all over. Susie sensed it too. The children trotted weakly behind Wee Jimmie, praying the dodo had hidden himself, but fearing the game was up.

The three of them arrived back in the farmyard and stopped suddenly. The shrill sound of squawking was coming from the outbuilding. Danny felt his legs might give way. He stared at the open doors. More squawking.

183

Loud yapping. What was happening in there? Any second now the dodo would rush out and pile straight into Wee Jimmie. Then it was curtains, finished, over!

In fact, it wasn't the dodo that ran out of the outbuilding but Shirley. She bolted through the double doors, yelping this time rather than yapping, and crashed straight into Wee Jimmie. He grabbed his dog, and she wriggled and twisted in his hands.

'Shirley! Calm down, lass!' said Wee Jimmie, holding the dog up in front of his face.

Shirley darted forward and sunk her teeth right into his juicy nose. Wee Jimmie cried out in pain and dropped the tiny dog. She ran under the van and cowered there. Quickly, Susie shut the outbuilding doors, trapping the dodo inside, as Granny Flora came running out of the house.

'What is it? What's happened to you,

Jimmie?' she asked, seeing blood trickling between his hands. He pulled them away to reveal his bitten nose.

'Oh good heavens! Whatever did that to you? Come in, let me patch that up!'

Wee Jimmie growled and protested, but Granny Flora led him inside and shut the door.

Exhausted, Danny looked over at Susie and smiled weakly.

'That went well,' he said.

Chapter 20

CRISIS

Granny wouldn't let Wee Jimmie go back in the outbuilding. After patching him up and giving him a small bowl of porridge, she insisted he go home to rest. She had to use her sternest Granny voice, and Roddy Aye had to back her up, pointing his knitting needles at Jimmie, who reluctantly gave up. He coaxed Shirley out from under the van and then, muttering something about coming back *very soon*, he drove off.

The children watched him go, and as soon as he was out of sight they snuck back into the outbuilding. The dodo was dozing in the cubbyhole. A small tuft of what had to be Shirley's fur was still trapped in his beak.

Danny stared at the dodo. The dodo opened one eye and stared back at Danny.

'Are you two not speaking any more?' Susie asked.

'He can't speak,' Danny huffed.

'But you used to be able to communicate, by looking at his eyes,' Susie said. 'That's what you said.'

The dodo opened his other eye and Danny looked into them and saw ... He wasn't sure what. He had brought the dodo here so they could have adventures together. He had fed him and cared for him. OK, maybe he should have given him a bit more fruit, but that was a tiny mistake, surely. It was going to be the best summer ever, but now it was all going terribly wrong. The dodo was strong-willed and defiant. He didn't listen to Danny. He didn't stay hidden. Danny had to lie for him. He had to eat porridge for him!

Danny turned away and walked slowly back to the house. Susie found him in his room, lying face down on his bed.

'I give up,' he said, rolling over and staring at the ceiling. 'I can't do this. Turns out I got it all wrong. Dodo wants to eat eggs and fruit, not taramasalata and custard creams. He wants to read travel guides in the paper, not Zac Hanaway! He's happier chucking washers at me than playing cracker Frisbee. Everything I thought I knew about him is wrong. This isn't an adventure any more, it's a nightmare! And now I've got a criminal from Glasgow trying to hunt him down. How can I possibly keep him safe now? I'm done with it. I give up! He can just go and live wild in the woods for all I care.'

Danny pulled a pillow over his head and lay perfectly still, perfectly miserable, perfectly defeated.

Susie, on the other hand, took out her note-book and read through her jottings. She stared at the clipping of the tropical beach that the dodo had torn out. She tapped her pencil against her top lip and furrowed her brow as she thought and thought.

'There has to be a reason for his actions,' she said. 'I think the egg and gooseberry eating was to get the nutrients he needed that he wasn't getting from the diet you gave him.'

'He likes Hula Hoops,' Danny mumbled from under the pillow.

'Well, maybe, but what about this?' said Susie.

Danny pushed the pillow off. She passed him the picture of the beach.

'You said that the bird picked through newspaper after newspaper, shredding them all, but saved that picture,' said Susie. 'Why?'

'I don't care any more,' said Danny, stuffing the picture into his pocket. 'He's just weird!'

'No!' said Susie. 'No one is just weird or naughty or anything for no reason. People only say that about things they don't understand. There is always something behind it. It's like this kid, Billy, at my school. He was picking on the children three years below him. Everyone thought he was a bully. Turns out he was being bullied by some big lads from the secondary school on his way home each day. He was scared and taking out his feelings on younger children.'

Danny groaned and sat up.

'Thanks for that interesting little story, but I don't see what you're getting at,' he said. 'Are you saying the dodo is being bullied?'

'I'm saying that there must be a reason behind all his behaviour of the last few days,' said Susie. 'You hoped the dodo would be a fun, exciting pet, but he's not. He's an animal and animals don't do stuff just for the heck of it. Something is driving him. Instinct or fear or hunger or ...'

'Lunch!' shouted Granny Flora.

The children plodded down to the kitchen.

Danny slumped over his soup, looking exhausted and miserable, while Susie feverishly made more notes in her jotter. In the corner, Roddy Aye knitted and smiled at no one in particular.

'Cheer up, Danny!' said Granny Flora, poking him with a pencil. 'Perhaps you can help me with my crossword while you eat?'

Danny mechanically ladled a spoonful of soup into his mouth, saying nothing.

'Three down,' said Granny Flora. 'The clue

is, longing for your native land. Eight letters ending in ick.'

Danny said nothing.

'HOMESICK,' said Susie, not looking up from her notebook.

'Ah yes, thanks, Susie,' said Granny Flora. 'How about this? Liberty – that's the clue. Seven letters starting with F.'

'FREEDOM,' said Susie, almost instantly.

'Oh, you're so good at this!' said Granny Flora. 'Come on, Danny, join in. Here we are. To stick at a task, to see it through. P E R something. Nine letters.'

'PERSEVERE,' said Susie, spooning up some soup.

'Quite right,' said Granny Flora. 'Good. There we are now. All done.'

With the crossword finished, she poked her pencil back into her hair. The rest of the lunch passed in silence.

'I can take you home now, Susie, if you like?' said Granny Flora. 'Save you walking and getting wet. It's pouring down.'

'Danny, I might go home,' Susie said. 'I need more time to puzzle our problem out, you know?'

Danny didn't seem to be listening. He had curled up in a chair by the stove, opposite Roddy, clutching a pot of taramasalata.

'OK, I'm off home,' said Susie. 'Bye.'

Danny said nothing. Tired and confused, he suddenly wished he could go home too.

He curled up tighter, aware of Roddy gazing at him gently from the other side of the stove, thinking about his home – the squidgy brown sofa where he watched films with his dad, the plant pots on the window sills, the comics scattered around his bedroom floor, his mum's walking boots by the back door. Home ... He knew every bit of it, every detail. He knew its smell, its warmth, the way the sun came through the kitchen window in the afternoons. He knew how it made him feel too. That feeling of home …

Suddenly, Danny went and grabbed the crossword. He sat back down, staring at it, his fingers tracing the words. FREEDOM, HOMESICK, PERSEVERE.

'That's it,' he murmured. 'That is it! Susie was right – there is a reason for all this. Of course, of course, of course! He just wants to go home!'

Chapter 21

HOMECOMING

Danny ran out into the rainy yard and into the outbuilding, rustling through the crispy drifts of shredded newspaper which still lay everywhere.

The dodo eyed him with suspicion. Panting, Danny grinned at the bird.

'I get it!' he said. 'You want to go home! *This* home.'

He waved the picture the dodo had ripped from the paper, showing a sunny beach with white sand.

'It's warm, sunny, nice! It's not Kinoussie in the rain. Of course! I should have got this sooner. I mean, I'd prefer to be on a tropical beach than here, and if that's your actual home, well then, of course you want to get back there!'

The guarded look seemed to dissolve from the dodo's eyes. Suddenly, they sparkled, they grew wider, they took all of Danny in. Then the dodo rushed out of his cubbyhole and threw himself at Danny, like a dog jumping up. He butted Danny's legs, he clacked his beak, he nibbled Danny's knees, he danced around him.

'Hey! Watch out!' said Danny, but he was laughing. He let his hands rest on the dodo's feathers, patting him and tickling him.

'I thought I could keep you in here and you'd be like a really cool pet, and it would be an adventure, me and my dodo. But you don't want to be in an outbuilding and you don't want to be a pet, either. You want to be here!'

Danny waved the beach picture again.

'Kinoussie's too cold, and it's too dangerous, especially with Wee Jimmie sniffing around,' he said. 'It's completely clear now. I thought the adventure was about keeping you. I was wrong. The adventure is getting you home.'

Danny repeated all this down the phone to Susie.

'Do you even know where his home is?' she said.

'No, but I know how to find out,' he said. 'Books! Research! Facts! Right, Susie? I'm coming round to your way of doing things!'

'I knew you would!' laughed Susie.

When she reappeared in the outbuilding, Danny and the dodo were sitting happily together in the cubbyhole, eating grapes.

'You want books, I've got books!' said Susie, heaving several heavy hardbacks out of her backpack. There was an encyclopaedia, an atlas and some books about wildlife.

The children began leafing through them, and Danny eventually found a page about dodos.

'They lived in Mauritius,' said Danny. 'Hang on, why do I know that name?'

'It's where flight MRU 3–96 goes every night, just before 10 p.m.,' said Susie. 'The only plane that flies over Kinoussie.'

Danny opened the atlas and found Mauritius, an island off the coast of Africa. Susie read from the encyclopaedia.

'Mauritius was settled by the Portuguese, then the Dutch.' She looked up, frowning thoughtfully. 'Is that how he got here? It was a Dutch ship that was wrecked on the island in Clootie Bay. Do you think it was on its way back from Mauritius when it got blown off course, with this bird's relatives on board?'

The dodo began clacking his beak excitedly, then hopped up on to the pile of books and jumped off.

'That has to be it!' said Danny. 'Surely now you believe he's a dodo, Susie! There's a logical explanation for him being here.'

'It's certainly an interesting theory. I will say that at least,' said Susie. 'But if he *is* from Mauritius, which is a really long way away, how are you going to get him back there?'

'Could he fly in a plane?' said Danny. 'Like on MRU 3–96?'

'How would you pay for the airfare? It

would be hundreds of pounds,' said Susie.

'What about if we try to smuggle him on to a boat?'

'Looking like he does? He's hardly going to blend in.'

'We could disguise him,' said Danny. 'A hat, a hoodie, maybe some little shoes.'

'With a giant yellow beak sticking out,' said Susie. 'I don't think that's going to work.'

'Could we mail him through the post?'

'Are you kidding? You'll never get a jiffy bag big enough.'

'Good point!' said Danny.

The children were so lost in thought they didn't notice that the dodo had climbed on to the back of the old, wonky armchair. Perched up there, he suddenly let out a loud squawk and then, beating his small wings frantically, he leaped off. Then he climbed up again, and jumped off again, wings beating rapidly.

'What's he doing?' Susie asked.

Danny stared at the bird, thinking hard.

'It's what he was doing in the woods, remember?' he said.

The dodo hauled himself on to the armchair and leaped off again, wings beating in a feathery flutter.

'Ohhh,' said Danny, smiling. 'I think I get it! That's *it*!'

'What?' said Susie.

'This, what he's doing! This is how he'll get home.'

'Nope, still don't get it!'

'Look!' Danny said. The dodo hurled himself off the chair again, stumpy wings batting the air.

'He will fly, of course!' said Danny, then he picked up a handful of shredded newspaper and tossed it into the air like confetti. The strips rained down like snow, the dodo squawked and the boy and the bird did a little hopping, beak-clacking dance of celebration.

Susie cleared her throat noisily.

'Sorry to kill the party,' she said. 'But, hello? Flying? Have you seen his wings?'

On cue, the dodo held them out from his sides and flapped them proudly, looking at one wing then the other. They were comically small, and out of proportion with his plump body, like the tiny, useless arms of a T-rex.

Susie read from the page about dodos.

'Look, it says here that dodos didn't need wings. There were no predators on Mauritius, so they lost the need and ability to fly.'

'Well, there *are* predators now,' said Danny. 'Wee Jimmie, for one, who would like to get his hands on the dodo and sell him. The dodo would never get home then. So if there is a predator, then there is a need to fly. Logical enough for you?'

'Maybe ... but look at the equipment,' said Susie, poking one of the dodo's wings with her pencil. The dodo grabbed the pencil in his beak and threw it aside.

'Doesn't matter!' said Danny. 'Remember, you said earlier that animals don't act for no reason, and there is always instinct or fear or whatever driving them. Well, that's it! He doesn't want to learn to fly just for fun. He's doing it to get home. His instinct can't be wrong. He wants to learn to fly, and I'm going to help him!'

The dodo clacked his beak triumphantly, then Danny and the bird stared at Susie.

'Now, are you in or are you out?' he asked.

Susie looked at Danny and the dodo. Then she closed her eyes, let out a huge sigh and shook her head.

'This goes against every rational instinct, and I might regret this, but ... IN!' she said, and was immediately knocked flying by an overexcited dodo, who pinned her to the floor under a pile of newspaper and clacked his beak six times.

'OK! OK!' she laughed. 'Get off me now!'

The dodo hopped down. Susie sat up and straightened her glasses.

'First things first,' she said. 'We need a name for this flying home plan.'

'That's easy,' said Danny. 'Operation Homecoming!'

Chapter 22

CONCUSSION

Danny, Susie and the dodo got to work on Operation Homecoming straightaway. Danny drew up an action plan.

1. Susie does research: flying, weather patterns, how migratory birds navigate
2. Susie organises research: buys new stationery, including binder, pencils, maybe a highlighter pen?
3. Danny works out where dodo can land in Mauritius
4. Draw up route map
5. Train dodo to fly (more detail coming later)
6. Make sandwiches etc. for journey
7. Dodo flies home!!!

Susie clapped her hands when she saw the finished list.

'A project! Great, my favourite thing! I'll go home and get started!' she said, but paused at the outbuilding doors.

'Danny, what about Wee Jimmie?' she said. 'What if he comes back before we've taught the dodo to fly?'

'Don't worry,' said Danny. 'I've got a plan for that too!'

He spent the rest of the afternoon and into the evening rigging up the outbuilding with security devices. The dodo watched quietly from the cubby as Danny positioned buckets full of water or cold porridge mixed with earth on strategic roof beams, with swinging ropes attached and trip wires across the floor. Before he cautiously picked his way out that evening, he hugged the dodo and smiled at him.

'Together we can do this!' Danny said. 'But you have to stay hidden and stay quiet, no matter who or what comes through those doors tonight.'

Then, carefully positioning a full bucket of water on a beam above the outbuilding doors, he went back to the house.

Danny was woken at 5 a.m. by a terrible clattering coming from the outbuilding, followed by a roar. He peeped quickly out of his window, but the farmyard was empty. He ran downstairs and outside.

The doors to the outbuilding were wide open and Danny could hear a man's muffled cursing coming from inside.

Danny peeked in. Wee Jimmie was standing in the middle of the outbuilding, wiping water from his face and wringing out his red woolly hat, the bucket now empty and lying on the floor.

The water above the doors had drenched him, but not stopped him.

Danny held his breath as Wee Jimmie looked around in the dim morning light then began inching towards the cubby where the dodo was hidden. His size-thirteen feet waded through the shredded newspaper. One step, two steps – THREE! His boot struck a trip wire, yanking it just enough to pull out a peg that held a large bucket, attached to a rope, up against the outbuilding roof; a large bucket loaded with porridge, compost and a few squirts of washing-up liquid. With a delicate swooshing sound it came swooping out of the gloom towards Wee Jimmie and struck him – **BANG** – right on his head. Danny winced as Wee Jimmie tottered and stumbled. He grabbed at the bucket to stop it striking him again and the cold porridge mix spilled all over him. Blinded by the gunk, he staggered around, groping at the mounds of junk in the outbuilding. All the while, the fine strips of newspaper began sticking to his slippery, porridgey, composty body until he resembled a dirty, shaggy yeti.

'Arrghh!' he roared. 'There! You're in there, aren't you!'

He pointed a shaky finger at the cubbyhole.

Danny gasped. The bucket had stunned Wee Jimmie but not knocked him out. Would nothing stop this man-mountain? Now, like a newspaper zombie, he lumbered towards the cubbyhole. Danny had told the dodo to stay quiet, stay hidden, but with a shudder he realised his advice was all wrong.

'DODO!' Danny yelled, sprinting into the outbuilding. 'RUN! *RUN!*'

The bird didn't hesitate. He raced out of

the cubbyhole, squawking angrily, and with a jump and a beat of his wings, he leaped into the air and kicked Jimmie squarely in his massive chest.

Danny watched as Wee Jimmie toppled straight backwards, like a tree being felled. Then, using his big belly as a springboard, the dodo bounced off Wee Jimmie and ran over to Danny.

Wee Jimmie lay silent for a few seconds, then began to stir and moan.

'Quick, Dodo, hide in the barn,' said Danny. The bird raced across the farmyard and disappeared into the huge, murky building on the other side. Just in time! Roddy Aye, who had fallen asleep by the fire, as he sometimes did, had heard the noise and woken Granny Flora.

They appeared in the doorway to the outbuilding. Wee Jimmie had staggered to his feet now and was walking shakily towards them, covered in porridge and soap bubbles and earth and a raggedy coat of old newspaper.

'I saw it!' he said, pointing at nothing in particular. The huge bump on his head where the bucket had hit him seemed to pulse red like a warning sign.

'The thing! Squawk he says! Oh, what kind of a beastie would live in a building like this, I wonder? His eyes, all yellow like fire!'

'Whatever has got into him?' said Granny Flora. 'He's making no sense.'

'He's had a bump on the head,' said Danny. 'Maybe it's damaged his brain?'

'I'm calling an ambulance,' said Granny Flora.

'When long-dead creatures come before our eyes again, then it's the time of miracles!' said Wee Jimmie. 'It runs, it squawks! See its grey feathers all feathery!'

Wee Jimmie paused and bent over, holding his head, wobbling a bit. Roddy Aye held on to his shoulder to steady him.

'The second coming of the bird!' Wee Jimmie said, straightening up and jabbing a finger into Roddy's chest. 'Squawk, squawk, my pretty! I sees you, oh yes. I see your great beak!'

Roddy helped Wee Jimmie out into the yard and plonked him down on a bench.

'No idea what he's going on about,' Danny said, raising his eyebrows. 'Must have been quite a blow!'

'Aye,' said Roddy, and then he glanced towards the barn.

The ambulance soon arrived and two paramedics jumped out.

'It's among us!' Wee Jimmie said, his eyes wild and then terribly confused. 'I saw the bird, the big bird!'

'That's right, settle down now, you saw a big bird,' said one of the ambulance crew soothingly, helping Wee Jimmie on to a stretcher. 'You've had a wee bang to your bonce, my friend. That's all.'

'I know its name,' said Wee Jimmie, sitting up again. 'They call it THE DODO!'

Danny winced at the d-word, but the ambulance man just patted Jimmie on his shoulder and laid him back down.

'That's right, you saw a dodo,' he muttered as the two of them lifted Jimmie into the back of the ambulance. 'Was he hanging out with his friends, the unicorn and the phoenix? Probably had a pixie in his pocket too, am I right?'

They slammed the ambulance doors shut.

'He has a touch of concussion, I think,' said the ambulance man as his teammate started the engine. 'He will probably need a few days in hospital, until the confusion and dizziness clears up. A dodo, eh? I like that! People say all sorts when they have concussion, but that's a new one on me. A dodo!'

'Aye,' said Roddy, and the ambulance drove away, blue lights flickering through the soft morning air.

Chapter 23

THEORY

News of the break-in and Wee Jimmie's accident spread fast. No secrets in Kinoussie, after all! When Susie came over for breakfast, Granny Flora had already been on the phone to Murdo McMurdo and Moira Storm. Willy McNeish had offered to buy Wee Jimmie a wheelbarrow as a get-well gift, and Donald in the Spar was going to put together a basket of food for him, including a couple of those turnips he'd got in, which weren't selling as well as expected.

'They say Wee Jimmie is ranting about seeing a giant bird and strange creatures,' Susie whispered. 'Will anybody guess?'

'I don't think so,' said Danny. 'Everyone thinks it's the bang on the head making him mad. But he did see the dodo. More of him than he wanted to! The dodo power-jumped off his belly!'

'He may forget that though,' said Susie. 'Memory loss is a common side effect of concussion. At least he's out of the way for a bit, but for how long?'

Granny Flora put the phone down and came back into the kitchen.

'They say he'll be in hospital for four days!' she said. 'You usually only have to be monitored for two days with concussion, but he's ranting so much about dodos and giant beaks and whatnot, they want to keep an eye on him for longer. He'll not be out before Sunday. What on earth was he doing in the outhouse first thing in the morning anyway?'

Danny and Susie said nothing. Roddy Aye, knitting by the fire, smiled faintly to himself.

'Oh well, this crossword won't get done on

its own,' said Granny Flora. She pulled the newspaper towards her and whipped a pencil out from her hair. The children slipped away.

While his gran had been busy ringing all her friends with the exciting news, Danny had escorted the dodo out of the barn and back to the outbuilding, and now he and Susie found him resting in his cubby.

'Ready for day one of Operation Homecoming?' Danny asked.

The dodo bobbed his head.

'Obviously, we got off to quite a dramatic start today,' said Danny. 'And now that Wee Jimmie has seen you we have to get a move on. He'll be out of hospital in four days and he's sure to come back. So we don't have long to get you flight ready. I don't dare move you, with the whole of Kinoussie aflutter after Wee Jimmie's accident. So we sit tight, work hard and get you out of here on Saturday night, under cover of darkness.'

The dodo blinked and stood very still.

'This morning – theory!' said Susie, opening her folder. It was crammed with maps, notes, scientific drawings, numbers and charts. She began explaining how migratory birds used the stars to navigate. How far Mauritius was, where the prevailing winds blew, what hazards the bird might encounter – planes, storms, geese. Danny handed her a map he'd created too, with the route marked on it and safe stopping-off points. Susie pinned it up on the wall.

'It's a pretty simple straight course,' she said, using a bamboo cane to point at the map. 'You fly south-eastwards, down through France, along the eastern edge of Italy, across the Med, then follow the Red Sea and it's just a short hop down from Somalia, across the sea to Mauritius.'

The dodo stared at the map.

'You'll have flight MRU 3–96 to start you off,' said Susie. 'Follow that at first, then use the map for guidance.'

'How long will it take him?' Danny asked. 'A couple of days?'

'What? Are you nuts? He isn't flying to Fort Plother for some groceries,' said Susie.

'Mauritius is over six thousand miles away!'

'So how long?'

'Well, a swallow can fly around two hundred miles a day, which would still take it thirty-two days to get there,' said Susie. 'This bird, on the other hand, could take double that. He can't feed while he's flying like swallows do, so he'll need to land and stock up and rest.'

Everyone was quiet for a while, as the scale of the task sunk in.

'The good news is, I've found just the place for him once he does get to Mauritius,' said Danny. 'There's a huge national park on the southwest of the island. Totally unspoiled and protected, with lush jungle. You'll love it there.'

The dodo clacked his beak excitedly.

'Best get on with the practical lessons then,' said Danny. 'We need to go outside, so let me check that no one is around.'

He slipped outside and saw Moira Storm pedalling slowly into the farmyard. She didn't see Danny, because her head was bent so low over the handlebars.

'Morning, Moira,' he called.

'Ah, it's you,' she said, once she had creakily got off her bike. 'I'm away off to visit Wee Jimmie in hospital with your gran.'

Danny nodded and counted silently under his breath: three, two, one.

'We'll need to be back by teatime,' she said. 'There's a storm coming.'

'There it is!' he whispered, and watched as Granny Flora helped Moira into her car and drove away. He ran back into the outbuilding.

'Phase two of Operation Homecoming clear to start. Repeat – clear to start!'

Within seconds, the dodo had raced outside and was standing in the sun, stretching his wings, eyes shining bright.

Chapter 24

CATAPULT

The plan for phase two of Operation Homecoming involved an old swing with a rusty frame in the far corner of Granny Flora's large garden.

The dodo pecked at the faded plastic seat like a child playing with its dinner.

'The idea is you sit on it like this,' said Danny, hopping on. 'Then you swing and jump off, like this!'

He leaped off when the swing was at the top of its arc and plopped down on the grass.

'Only you fly down,' he added. 'Got it?'

The bird tried hopping up, but either bashed into the swing seat or tumbled straight over it. Eventually, Danny and Susie had to lift him on to the swing, by holding hands under his fat belly and gently placing him in the seat.

'Now hold on!' said Danny. 'I'm going to start pushing.'

The dodo used his huge strong beak to grip the chain as Danny pushed again and again.

'Now, when you get to the top on this next push, jump!' he called.

And the dodo did. The jumping bit went quite well, actually. The flying down bit? Not so much.

The dodo landed roughly on his feet, ran a few steps, tripped, rolled head over heels and ended up in a bush.

The children loaded the dodo on to the swing again, but the same clumsy landing happened, and there was no evidence of any flying whatsoever, just a frantic flutter of wings before a disappointing crash.

Then Danny tried lobbing crackers as the dodo jumped off, thinking he might be inspired to fly towards each one and snap it up, just like when they played cracker Frisbee. It didn't work. The dodo jumped, beak open, and missed the cracker, before tumbling down on the grass.

Danny scratched his head and looked around, thinking hard. The sun was shining, no hint of the storm Moira had predicted, and Granny had hung her washing on the line. It included, he noticed, several of Moira's surgical stockings, which Granny had agreed to run through the wash on a special surgical stocking cycle that her machine had.

'Ah ha!' said Danny, grabbing a few of the stretchy, wrinkly, flesh-coloured stockings off the line. 'Feel how stretchy these are!'

Susie grimaced before tugging at one of the stockings.

'Gross!' she said. 'What does she use these for?'

'I dunno,' shrugged Danny. 'Granny Flora says they help keep everything in place, but never mind that. Concentrate on how stretchy they are.'

'They are very stretchy, yes,' said Susie, nervously picking at one again. 'What's your plan?'

'A catapult!' said Danny, his eyes shining. 'Stretch a couple of these *things* between those two trees over there and launch the dodo into the air.'

The dodo tugged at one of the stockings with his beak. It snapped out of Susie's hand and pinged him in the face. He squawked.

'That could work!' she said. 'If we get the angle right and the correct tension, we can fire him up and along, giving him more time to start flying. Jumping off the swing is too downwards.'

By knotting several stockings together, the children soon had a long length of stretchy material, like a big pink elastic band, which they tied between two stunted hawthorn trees.

'How far do you reckon he'll go?' said Susie. 'I mean, he won't hit that big tree over there, will he?'

'No!' said Danny. 'He'll be flying anyway. He can just fly over it.'

Danny pulled the stockings back into a deep U shape, hanging off them with all his weight to keep them at full stretch, and Susie quickly ushered the dodo in, so his white feathery tail was just touching the taut loop. Then she got out of the way and yelled: 'Three, two, one – FIRE!'

Danny let go.

The surgical stockings pinged towards the two trees, scooping the dodo off his feet and firing him out. There was barely time for the bird to flap his wings. He was speeding along in a low arc towards the big tree in the distance and then, suddenly, he was splattered against it, like a gnat on a car headlight.

'OOHHH,' said Danny and Susie together.

'That wasn't really flying,' said Susie. 'That was hurling.'

By the time they reached the dodo, he had plopped backwards on to the ground and was lying there, perfectly still, eyes closed.

Danny knelt beside the bird, patting his feathers, searching for a heartbeat.

'He's not dead, is he?' said Susie, nervously.

Suddenly, those golden eyes pinged open and, with a triumphant squawk, the dodo leaped to his feet, rolled Danny on to his back with one shove of his plump, feathery chest

230

and began running around him in circles.

'He's fine!' said Susie, slightly surprised. 'Phew! He's fine.'

'Of course he is!' said Danny. 'He's supposed to be extinct, remember? He's a fighter!'

The children tried again and again, angling the surgical stockings to get the dodo higher into the air and tying them at different places on the trees. The dodo eagerly tried to fly each time. He landed once in the branches of the big tree, once in a puddle and once against the fence of the chicken coop, which gave all the hens flashbacks and made them cluck madly with panic. On the final attempt, the knot in the stockings slipped and came undone. With a thud, the dodo fell backwards on to Danny's lap.

Danny checked his watch. They had missed lunch, it was already mid-afternoon.

'Granny Flora might be home soon from

visiting Wee Jimmie,' he said. 'Come on, you, up you get. Best get you inside again.'

'We didn't make very good progress today,' said Susie.

'Don't worry, we'll do more tomorrow, he'll get there,' said Danny, stroking the dodo's head. 'The only way is up, right?'

And that gave Susie an idea.

Back in the outbuilding, she made a few notes and sketches in her jotter.

'We'll use a trampoline,' she said finally, showing Danny and the dodo her drawings. 'To send the dodo vertically into the air. The higher the better, so that he has time to beat his wings and fly back down. Where a swing and a catapult have failed, a trampoline could work.'

'Only problem is, we don't have a trampoline,' said Danny.

'I know, but there is one at Scotland's smallest campsite. There are pitches for one and a half tents and the trampoline. That's all,' said Susie. 'If we can get the dodo down there, we can sneak in when the campers go out for the day and practise!'

With the plan in place, Susie went home. Danny got the dodo his dinner, then went indoors for his.

'We saw Wee Jimmie,' said Granny Flora. 'He'll definitely not be out of hospital until Sunday, they reckon. He's saying he wants to come back and check over our outbuilding. Something about a creature in there.'

Danny gulped. He could feel the warmth draining from his cheeks.

'I'm sure he's not right in the head though,' Granny Flora laughed. 'That blow knocked all the sense out of him. There's no creature in there, after all, just a lot of junk.'

Next morning, Danny went to find the dodo.

'I have to get you to the campsite without anyone guessing you are you,' Danny explained as the bird gobbled up his breakfast of eggs and banana. 'So you're going to wear a disguise.'

Danny wrapped his hoodie around the dodo, sleeves dangling, and then pulled a mass of fluffy material out of his pocket.

'This is my special Scottish hottie bottie cover, shaped like a Westie dog,' Danny said. It was fluffy and white, with a cute dog's head on top and a hollow body for the hot-water bottle. 'I'm going to put it on your head!'

The dodo's face peered out from the fluffy cover, with the dog's head sitting on top.

'Perfect!' said Danny. 'No one will ever guess. Possibly ...'

Once Susie had rung to say the campers had left, Danny helped the dodo into the pram and pushed as fast as he could towards the village centre. He raced past Sheila Creasy, shouting he was dying to hear about the old days and would be right back. Sheila grinned and waved her pipe, distracted, not noticing the strange creature in the pram. Danny dashed past the Spar, where the sign outside now read: TURNIPS - BUY ONE, GET TWO FREE, WHILE STOCKS LAST!

Then he found Susie, hiding behind a bush near the entrance to Scotland's smallest campsite.

'No one saw us,' puffed Danny.

'Good,' said Susie, staring at the dodo. 'What is he supposed to look like?'

'Like a dog!' said Danny.

'A dog with a beak?'

'He's wearing my hottie bottie cover.'

'Hottie bottie?' said Susie, starting to giggle. 'Did you just say hottie ...'

'Shut up!' said Danny. 'Be sensible. We've got work to do.'

The dodo clacked his beak at Susie, like he was telling her off.

'All right, you two,' she muttered. 'Talk about a sense of humour failure …!'

Susie checked for any cars or people, then they ran up the track to the campsite, neither of them spotting the wheelbarrow by the entrance gate. Then Danny whipped his hoodie off the dodo, who sprang out of the pram and ran towards the trampoline.

The dodo took to trampolining immediately, springing down hard with his broad, yellow feet and pinging up into the air, clacking ecstatically. With each jump and descent he beat his wings, harder and faster and longer. Did he manage to hover, for a split second, at the top of those leaps? Danny couldn't be sure, but maybe.

The children watched the dodo bouncing around and then couldn't resist the urge to join him. Soon all three of them were pinging up and down, laughing and beak-clacking and whooping. Danny kept daring Susie and the dodo to go higher, higher, higher, until all three of them were clearing the top of the safety net around the trampoline and could see the campsite driveway.

Up they went, again and again, three heads bobbing for a split second above the thick netting, then down again. And that's just what Willy McNeish saw as he stood by the campsite entrance. He'd come for his wheelbarrow, which he'd noticed at the side of the track – must have left it there some time ago – and he was struggling to believe his eyes. Three heads appeared above the trampoline for a split second – a boy with blond hair, a girl with a straight dark bob

237

and a, what was it? A dog with a beak and short wings?

The three of them bounced like this, with Willy watching, puzzled, for some time before Danny spotted him.

'Abort, abort, abort!' he screeched, crashing down and yanking Susie after him. 'Willy is over there!'

Susie landed on him and the dodo crashed down on top of them both, creating a triple pile-up.

'Quick!' Danny hissed. 'Into those woods. Hide!'

Susie lifted up the safety net and the three of them scrabbled out and raced into the woods. They flung themselves down behind a tree, and then Danny peered out.

'Has he gone?' Susie whispered.

'He looks confused,' said Danny. 'He's checking the trampoline and scratching his head. OK, he's going now. He's picked up his wheelbarrow. He's gone. Phew!'

'What if Willy tells?' Susie said. 'There's no crime in Kinoussie, so a couple of kids and a weird dog-bird breaking into a trampoline is big news. Sergeant MacDuff might get involved.'

'Oh great, the police!' said Danny. 'This was your idea. You said the coast was clear.'

'How was I to know Willy would come in search of his wheelbarrow?' said Susie.

'You should have done your research,' said Danny. 'I thought you loved research!'

Before Susie could reply, the dodo waddled calmly between the two children. He reached his small wings out, so that the tip of each one touched each child, and shook his head.

'He's right,' said Danny. 'We don't have time to fight. Let's go home and get him hidden again.'

Chapter 25

FLIGHT MRU 3-96

The dodo was tired from trampolining and took a long nap after lunch. Danny didn't dare go back to Scotland's smallest campsite for more bouncing that afternoon, so instead he spent some time looking through all their notes and sticking pictures of swallows and geese and other birds that migrate all over the dodo's cubby, to keep him motivated.

Danny went in for dinner feeling a little concerned. Would the dodo be ready to fly by Saturday night? It was already Thursday and Danny wasn't sure that they'd made any real progress.

He sat down at the kitchen table. Roddy Aye had just finished off some knitting by the stove. He stood up and put on his coat, ready to go home.

'Bye, Roddy,' said Danny.

Roddy patted his shoulder and smiled. 'Aye!' he said.

'Why does Roddy never say anything except aye?' Danny asked his grandmother, once Roddy had left.

'Have I not told you before?' she said. 'It's very sad. When Roddy was a young man he fell in love with a lassie from the next village, and she seemed to like him too. He asked her to marry him, thinking she'd say yes, but she said no. Apparently, she had another chap down in Fort Plother she was sweet on. Poor Roddy was so shocked and heartbroken by that no that he couldn't speak again. The only word he would say was aye. I suppose because aye was the word he hoped she'd say.'

Granny Flora stared out of the window.

'Such a shame,' she said. 'Roddy had a beautiful voice too. He was famous around these parts for his singing. Strong men would weep to hear Roddy sing, but all that stopped when that lassie said no to him.'

Danny stared into his water glass and thought about this. No could be a terrible word, it was true. No you can't do this. No you can't go there. No you can't go home. No you can't fly. It was better to say yes to life, yes to everything, to hope and to adventure and to porridge. No wait, not to porridge, but all the other stuff, for sure.

After dinner, Danny settled in front of the TV. He was only half watching it though. His brain was still puzzling and niggling at how to help the dodo fly. The trampoline had been great practice, but now it was out of bounds. The stockings and swing really hadn't worked. What could he try tomorrow? Time was running out. Wee Jimmie would be out of hospital in a couple of days. Think! Think!

Suddenly, Danny realised that a nature programme was on, about seabirds that nest on high cliffs. Soon after hatching, the chicks had to jump into the sea, without being able to fly, to join their parents in the water below. He watched, wide-eyed, as the tiny fluffy chicks launched themselves off the super-high cliffs then plummeted down to the sea, their small, scrawny wings outstretched to help them glide. It gave Danny an idea. He snuck outside and found the dodo dozing in his cubbyhole.

'Rather than pinging you up, we need to push you off!' he said. 'I've just worked it out. That's what we'll do tomorrow.'

The dodo clacked his beak and Danny stroked his smooth back.

Then Danny glanced at his watch. It was almost 10 p.m.; time for flight MRU 3–96 to fly over.

'Quick! Come outside,' he said. 'Don't worry, Granny's asleep by the fire. Come on. You need to see this plane. It goes to Mauritius. Home!'

They scurried quietly out into the garden and sat on the grass, eyes pointed up to see the flashing lights on the wing tips of flight MRU 3–96 as it flew across the night sky.

'When you leave on Saturday, follow this plane,' Danny said. The dodo studied the plane silently, but Danny wasn't looking up at it. He was gazing quietly at the bird instead. Those words echoed around his head as the dodo stared up at the plane. 'When you leave on Saturday ...'

Chapter 26

BARN

'We're relocating to the barn for today's lesson,' Danny said to Susie and the dodo the next morning. 'There's a high platform in it, reached by a ladder. You're going to jump off it, Dodo!'

The dodo spun around three times.

'He's stress spinning,' said Susie. 'Are you sure this is a good idea?'

'He understands that we have to do this. It's OK,' said Danny. 'I saw a nature programme with these little chicks flinging themselves off a cliff. It's how they begin learning to fly, and how they get off the dangerous rocks and into the sea, to safety. If it works for them, it could work for the dodo.'

'Fine, but getting the dodo up there is not

going to be easy,' she said. 'He weighs a lot! Shall we try the catapult again?'

'Too dangerous. Plus, I think Moira took her stockings back,' said Danny. 'Could we throw him?'

'No, he's way too heavy for that,' said Susie. 'Perhaps some kind of winch mechanism, with a pulley system and a basket for him to sit in?'

'Where are we going to get all that from?' said Danny. 'Next you'll be suggesting we just get ourselves a rocket and fire him out of it.'

Luckily, there was no need for pulleys or rockets. The dodo had hopped up on to the first rung of the ladder and, using his huge, immensely powerful beak to grip on to the rung above, was slowly climbing up.

'That's my bird!' laughed Danny as the dodo slowly went higher. 'He has all the answers!'

'Get behind him though, he could slip,' said Susie.

Danny hopped up the ladder and put his arms around the bird protectively. Eventually, they made it to the top and edged out on to the platform. The floor of the barn, which was strewn with dusty straw, looked a long way down. Susie squinted up at them.

'What now?' she said.

'He jumps!' said Danny, but the dodo didn't move. He was staring at the floor below, swaying a bit, obviously nervous.

'Come on, Dodo, it's easy,' said Danny. 'Jump, flap, fly! Ready?'

Still the bird wouldn't move.

'Susie!' Danny shouted down. 'Spread some hay out so the dodo has something soft to land on.'

Susie scattered the hay and began sneezing as dust rose up from it.

'OK, I'm going
to count to three,'
said Danny, stand-
ing very close to the
dodo now.

The bird's claws
curled around the
edge of the wooden
platform.

'One!' said Danny.

The dodo stared
ahead and gulped.

'Two!' said Danny.

He held his wings
out, ready.

'THREE!' roared
Danny.

The dodo beat
his wings, whacking
Danny in the face.

He fell backwards, blinking. By the time he had sat up and scrabbled to the edge of the platform, the bird was down on the ground.

'Are you OK?' Danny shouted, rubbing his eyes. 'Susie, did he fly?'

Susie couldn't say. She was still too busy sneezing. She had yanked off her glasses and was wiping her streaming eyes with her sleeve.

Danny clambered down the ladder.

'He must have flown!' he said. The dodo seemed unhurt and happy.

'Shall we do it again? This time we'll film it! Susie, have you got your phone with you? Mine's bust.'

She reached into her pocket and, sneezing, passed her phone to Danny.

'I can barely stop sneezing,' she moaned. 'I need clean air. I just need to get outside until my nose calms down.'

Danny propped the phone against a straw bale and once again climbed the ladder behind the dodo.

'Now, this time, we won't miss a thing!' he said as the dodo stood on the edge of the platform, like a diver preparing to jump.

'Jump, flap, fly! Remember?' Danny said, crossing his fingers behind his back for luck.

The dodo took a deep breath, looked ahead of him and stretched out his wings. Danny stared, saw him beat his tiny wings, then noticed an enormous black spider crawling across the floor near the dodo's foot. Danny leaped up in fright, and when he looked back, the dodo was gone. Once again, he'd missed him jump.

'Never mind, I was filming it!' he said, racing back down the ladder and grabbing the phone.

He played the recording. The phone must have slipped. There was twenty seconds of footage of the barn roof and the sound of Danny screaming, but that was it.

'I don't believe it!' he sighed, then suddenly Susie rushed inside, a very clear look of panic on her face.

'The police!' she hissed. 'They're here!'

Chapter 27

POLICE

Danny hid the dodo behind some straw bales and then peeped around the barn door. A police officer was talking to Granny Flora at the front door. Danny could only hear fragments of their conversation.

'… some kind of dog with two children?', 'a trampoline', 'most unusual …', 'off into the woods'.

Granny Flora kept shaking her head, then the police officer went inside.

'What are they doing?' Danny whispered.

'That's Sergeant MacDuff,' said Susie. 'He's the only police officer around here. Everyone knows him. Your gran has probably invited him in for porridge.'

Ten long minutes later the policeman emerged and, wishing Granny Flora a cheery goodbye, drove off.

Danny let out a long breath.

'This isn't good!' said Susie. 'If anyone makes a connection between what Wee Jimmie says he saw and what Willy McNeish saw when he collected his wheelbarrow, we could be in trouble.'

Danny shook his head.

'Everyone thinks Wee Jimmie is still dazed and talking rubbish,' he said. 'And Willy is so forgetful, he's probably already forgotten what he told the police.'

'I suppose so,' said Susie. 'But he obviously told them something ...'

The dodo toddled quietly up to them and glanced nervously into the yard.

'It's all getting a bit complicated,' said Susie. 'Wee Jimmie, the police, they're all looking for the bird now. Plus, it's Friday today and he's meant to be flying tomorrow night, and we don't even know if he *can* fly yet!'

'We have to have faith,' said Danny, his eyelid twitching nervously. 'I trust you, Dodo, right?'

The dodo clacked his beak confidently.

'We have more time today to practise and all of tomorrow too,' said Danny.

'Oh, that reminds me!' said Susie. 'I've got to help Mum do her twice-yearly clean of Moira Storm's house tomorrow. She's too bent over to reach the high stuff! It means I can't come over tomorrow for training.'

'OK,' said Danny, his eyelid twitching a bit more. 'We'll be all right. Me and my dodo. We've got this!'

Susie looked worried.

'I promise I'll make it to the location for take-off though,' she said.

'We'll be ready!' said Danny, smiling faintly, the amount of work he had to do, alone, with the dodo to make him flight-ready for tomorrow slowly seeping in.

'Remember to feed him plenty of fresh eggs later,' Susie said. 'He needs the protein! And make sure he has some rest this afternoon. He mustn't get worn out before the big flight. Pack his bag, won't you – the list of everything that goes in it is on the side of the cubbyhole. And, well, that's it, really. Right, OK, fine. Good luck then!'

Susie turned to leave but the dodo blocked

her way. She crouched down in front of him and, very gently, the dodo leaned towards her and straightened her glasses with his beak. Susie reached out her hand and touched the bird softly on his leathery grey face, then she walked away.

'I'm not crying, by the way,' she muttered. 'It's the dust!'

Chapter 28

FIGHT

Danny planned to spend the afternoon practising with the dodo in the barn, but when he popped inside for lunch, his granny was frowning.

'There you are!' she said. 'We've had Sergeant MacDuff here. Something about two wee kiddies and a funny-looking dog using the trampoline at the campsite.'

Danny stayed silent.

'I don't want to hear your excuses,' said Granny Flora, pushing her hearing aid deeper into her ear. 'I don't know about the funny dog, but seeing as the only two children for miles around are you and Susie, I'm not surprised Sergeant MacDuff came straight here.'

Danny kept quiet.

'There's no point trying to deny it!' said Granny Flora.

Danny didn't say anything.

'That's enough of your cheek, Danny!' said Granny Flora, really quite cross now. 'You know you can't use trampolines that don't belong to you, even in Kinoussie, which is a very friendly place. I want you to stay in this afternoon and do something quiet. Maybe some drawing, like you used to when you were smaller. Or the crossword or knitting with Roddy there, instead of tearing about the village, bouncing on other people's things!'

Suddenly, Danny erupted.

'No!' he shouted. 'I can't stay in this afternoon! I've got things I have to do!'

'Yes, like behaving yourself and not causing trouble!' said Granny Flora sternly.

'I'm not causing trouble, I'm trying to help

someone, someone I care about,' said Danny. 'Surely you approve of that.'

'Whatever your motives, you can't break into the campsite!' said Granny Flora.

'That's what Wee Jimmie did here!' said Danny, flushing red. 'He broke into the outbuilding. And he's got a criminal past, but you seem to forgive him that.'

'Criminal past? What are you talking about?' she said.

'I read it in the newspaper!'

'You can't trust the papers!' said Granny Flora. 'I don't know what you read, but I can tell you Wee Jimmie is a very nice, helpful man who does a lot for people around here. I don't know anything about his past and that's fine by me.'

'But when your own grandson wants to be helpful, take responsibility like you always go on about, and do something for someone in need, he gets told off,' said Danny. 'Because I'm not part of Kinoussie life? Because I don't belong here? Is that it?'

Granny Flora looked shocked. Danny stormed upstairs and slammed his bedroom door. No secrets in Kinoussie! Everyone looks after everyone else! Ha! What rubbish. Danny had a secret – the dodo – and Wee Jimmie probably had a whole van-ful of nasty secrets too. Yet all the Kinoussie folk, including Danny's gran, thought he was great.

Danny sulked in his bedroom for a few hours and then tried to sneak back out to the barn, to see if the dodo had practised some more. Each time though, his granny appeared in the yard, calling his name, and finally forced him to have a two-hour knitting lesson with Roddy. Finally, at about 8.30 p.m., Granny Flora nodded off over her crossword and Danny was able to sneak the dodo some eggs.

'I am *so* sorry!' he whispered. 'Did you get any more practice done in the barn? Granny wouldn't let me out of her sight! It's OK though, we have time to work on your flying tomorrow. I mean, it's nearly there, isn't it? You definitely did fly down in the barn, didn't you? There's nothing to worry about, is there?'

The dodo beat his wings briefly. Danny smiled, but felt uneasy. The evening seemed to be unusually cool, even for Scotland. He heard the wind blowing outside, making the barn doors bang.

'Tomorrow is the big day then,' said Danny. He stroked the dodo's wings softly.

'Sleep tight, rest up and I'll see you again in the morning.'

He felt a few splashes of rain on his face as he walked back across the farmyard. He put his hood up.

The phone rang as soon as he got inside.

'Danny?' It was Susie, but it barely sounded like Susie. Her voice was trembling, stuttering.

'What is it?' he said.

'He's out, Danny!' said Susie. 'Wee Jimmie discharged himself from hospital. I was just sitting with Sheila Creasy outside her house while she talked about the old days, and we saw his van go past, swerving about the place. He's heading your way. Nothing can stop him. What will you do?'

Danny's eyes flashed around the room, not seeing anything.

'Danny?' said Susie.

'We stick with the plan, just bring it forward a night,' he said.

'But is Dodo ready? Can he make it?'

'He has to be ready,' said Danny. 'He has to make it. Wee Jimmie knows he's in there and he won't stop to make friends with him.

263

He'll grab him, sell him, who knows what. Dodo has to fly tonight!'

He hung up the phone and raced outside. Sitting in the dim corner by the stove, unseen by Danny, Roddy Aye nodded slowly.

Danny sped into the outhouse and began hurriedly packing a small, slim backpack with food, a map, a little flask of fresh water.

'We have to leave!' he told the dodo, helping him put the backpack on. 'Don't panic, but Wee Jimmie is coming and he'll catch you and kill me, or the other way around, or all of it. Do you think you can start your flight home tonight? Are you ready?'

The sound of van tyres screeching over gravel made Danny spin round.

He raced over to the doors and peered through. Wee Jimmie's van had skidded badly and ended up on Granny Flora's patio, smashing into a decorative terracotta pig that sat there. The pig's head had come clean off and was now rolling across the farmyard towards the outbuilding.

Danny saw Wee Jimmie get down from his van. His head was bandaged so he looked like he was wearing a white hat. He tottered and swayed on his feet, then reached into the van for something. What was it? Danny didn't wait to find out.

'We have to get out now, Dodo, come on!' he said, ushering the bird out of his cubby, through the piles of junk. Too late! There was a squeak as the double doors were flung open. A man's huge silhouette was framed against the pale evening light.

'There you are!' Wee Jimmie roared, pointing something long and threatening at Danny and the dodo. Danny stood in front of the bird, protecting him.

'You've broken my terracotta pig!'

It was Granny Flora's voice, coming from the farmyard. 'Wee Jimmie, you should be in hospital. Get back there this instant!'

'Don't tell me what to do!' Wee Jimmie bellowed, spinning round unsteadily on his feet. 'You can't boss me about. I'm going to be rich! I won't be cleaning your gutters and gotters and getters once I get my hands on that thing in there.'

'There's nothing in there, Jimmie,' Granny Flora pleaded. 'It's the bang on your head, making you see things!'

Jimmie blinked lazily, like he'd forgotten why he was there, then raised the long thing in his hands and pointed it at Granny Flora. Danny shuddered. It was an air rifle.

'Dear turnips, he's gone mad!' she shrieked.

'I'm calling the police.'

Danny heard her running back inside. She had no idea that he wasn't safe indoors, no clue that he was inside the outbuilding, about to face down a gigantic, bald, gun-toting maniac with a criminal past and a nasty head injury.

Wee Jimmie snorted, like he was remembering an old joke, then lolloped into the outbuilding.

'Come out, come out, wherever you are,' he chanted. 'Where's my bird! Where's my prize! You fat beauty, you're going to make Wee Jimmie rich. No more odd jobs for Jimmie. Ha!'

Wee Jimmie swayed wildly and slumped into a tower of boxes beside him. The top one slipped off the pile and sent its contents skittering across the floor towards Danny. He glanced down. Old vinyl LPs! Then he saw one of the sleeves: *Songs to Make You Weep, Sung by Roddy Dunoon*. Records of Roddy singing, before he stopped speaking. Who knew they were stuffed away here in the outbuilding?

Wee Jimmie righted himself and squinted through the half-light of the outbuilding. He stared at Danny and frowned.

'Is it behind you, that bird?' he asked. 'Don't, don't, just don't bother trying to hide it. It's mine now, so just step aside and let me take it.'

Danny glanced behind at the dodo, then back at Wee Jimmie slowly coming towards them. Jimmie slipped on one of the LPs.

'Time for a little game of Frisbee!' said Danny. 'Ready, Dodo!'

The dodo threw first, grabbing an LP and sending it straight into Wee Jimmie's belly. Danny threw another disc, which

skimmed past his eyebrows. They hurled LPs at Wee Jimmie so fast he barely saw them. They were bouncing off his huge body, **POW, POW, POW,** until one hit his left hand; the one with the HAT tattoo, the one holding the air rifle! It made Wee Jimmie's arm fly up. His fingers jerked. He pulled the trigger.

BANG!

Then it all happened so fast.

The rifle fired up into the outbuilding roof, the pellet passing perfectly through the rope attached to one final bucket hanging from a beam, put there by Danny for when Wee Jimmie first broke into the outbuilding.

Danny and the dodo watched the rope ping apart, then the bucket descended straight down – and **THUMP!**

It struck Wee Jimmie clean on the head. For the second time in a handful of days, he was knocked out. He fell backwards on the outbuilding floor, completely unconscious.

Chapter 29

BREAK-IN

There was no time to celebrate. Danny vaulted over the fallen figure of Wee Jimmie, the dodo racing along behind, and the two of them zoomed off towards the coast. The dodo was wearing his backpack and Danny had a bag too, packed and ready with a wrench, map, padlock and matches, plus food and water.

'Remember the plan? We're going to the lighthouse,' Danny panted. 'It's high, so it will be the perfect starting-off point.'

The wind was blowing fiercely now, so Danny didn't hear Moira, cycling along the road. Moira didn't even notice the dodo; her eyes were wild. She was heading to the farm-house to warn Granny Flora.

'There's a storm coming!' she shrieked, but Danny and the dodo didn't turn back. They carried on running, the rain stinging their faces, until they arrived at the old disused lighthouse, just down the coast from Clootie Bay.

Danny shook the padlock on the door. It was rusty and ancient. He took the wrench from his bag and struck it several times. Finally, the padlock fell open.

'Inside, quick!' he said, shoving the dodo into the lighthouse and securing the door on the inside with the padlock he had in his bag.

Then boy and dodo climbed and climbed, up and round in a twisting spiral, until they reached the top. Here, the old lantern, its oil lamp sitting inside a case of mirrors, sat motionless. A door led out to a balcony that stretched right around the top of the tower.

By now, Danny and the dodo were out of

breath, soaked and shaken. Danny took off his hoodie and used it to towel dry the dodo a little. He glanced out. The sea was stormy. The wind whistled around the lighthouse. For once, Moira was right. It was a storm all right! Danny realised with horror that the thick cloud and rain would stop the dodo from spotting flight MRU 3–96.

He looked at his watch. Still twenty minutes until 10 p.m., when the plane would fly over. *Don't panic, don't panic.* The storm could blow over by then; storms were often violent but short up here in West Scotland.

Danny took some food from his bag and handed it to the dodo, then together they studied the map of the flight route one last time, before tucking it in the dodo's small backpack. Danny checked his watch again.

'Ten minutes until take-off!' he whispered to the dodo. 'Are you ready?'

The bird shifted a little on the spot, but his eyes were calm.

'You are amazing,' said Danny. 'I know you can do this.'

The two gazed at each other for a moment, then the sound of people, cars and shouting drifted up through the storm from below.

Danny went out on to the balcony. The wind tugged at his hair. He peered over the edge. A police car had arrived and Granny Flora, Moira Storm and Roddy Aye got out. Then Sergeant MacDuff yanked Wee Jimmie from the back seat. He still had his white bandage on, but was also in handcuffs. Then he saw Willy McNeish, who was heading for the lighthouse too, pushing a wheelbarrow and looking a bit confused, and behind him …

'Susie!' Danny yelled, waving from the balcony.

'Are you OK?' she shouted from below. Her

275

voice sounded faint, the storm was at its peak now. 'Stick to the plan, Danny! I'll try to keep them back!'

There was no way Susie could keep a policeman and a crowd of grown-ups from barging their way into the lighthouse, but she tried, standing in front of the door, shouting through the wind that they weren't allowed to go up – it was breaking and entering private property!

'All right now, Susie, stand aside,' said the sergeant.

He shook the door but the padlock inside held fast, then he lumbered back to his car to get a crowbar.

Danny could hear the sound of the door being forced open. Its creaks and groans drifted up the winding staircase and reached him and the dodo as they sat by the unlit lantern.

Still five minutes before MRU 3–96 flew over, but what if the clouds didn't part in time?

'I have to do something, to help you find your way!' he muttered. 'In case you can't see the plane!'

Danny grabbed his bag and tipped it out, searching through the scattered contents. Then the dodo picked up the torch lying on the floor and dropped it in Danny's lap. He flicked it on and the dodo grabbed it back, holding it in his beak and spinning around three times on the spot.

'Are you stress spinning?' Danny asked.

The dodo went round again. The torch threw a beam around the lighthouse balcony. Round and round it went; a beam of light …

'Of course!' shrieked Danny. 'A light to help you home. I'll light the lighthouse!'

He leaped up, but then stood stock-still.

He could hear the door straining down below, and then a huge clatter and a roar as the sergeant managed to push it in!

'They've broken through the door, Danny,' Susie yelled, her voice clearer now, rising up the stairs.

Danny started to shake. He had to light the lighthouse, but the policeman was inside now. He could hear footsteps beginning to climb the stairs.

'Don't move, son!' yelled Sergeant MacDuff. 'We're coming for you.'

The dodo squawked in alarm and hopped from one yellow foot to the other.

'What are we going to do, Dodo?' Danny said, plunging his fingers into his hair. 'They're coming! I can hear them!'

But then he realised he could hear something else too. Faint at first, then, as the wind dropped, louder. A sweet, melancholy song. A man's voice, pure as a bell and packed with feeling. The footsteps stopped on the stairs below. The rain stopped too. Only the sound of Roddy Aye, singing on the grass outside the lighthouse, could be heard rippling through the cool Scottish night.

Danny peered over the edge of the balcony and saw Roddy, his eyes lifted to the sky, singing and singing. Granny Flora had her hand over her mouth, in silent, tearful surprise. Then Sergeant MacDuff appeared, stumbling across the grass. He had left the lighthouse and come to see Roddy singing. Now he was rooted to the spot, listening, his hankie gripped in one hand.

'*Songs to Make You Weep*, that was Roddy's album,' muttered Danny. 'Songs to buy you some time, more like. Thank you, Roddy! I definitely owe you one!'

Danny dashed back inside the lighthouse

and opened the mirrored casing of the lantern. Then he put a match to the ancient wick at its heart. It lit instantly. He closed its doors and watched as the mirrors magnified the flame to create a huge beam.

'It's not turning!' said Danny. 'Never mind, I'll do it myself. When it's time to jump, I'll find you and light your way.'

The dodo nodded and looked out to sea. He sniffed the salty air. The clouds, speeding along in the wind, broke to show the moon. Then stars appeared, studding the night sky like tiny jewels.

'The clouds are blowing away, Dodo, just in time,' said Danny. 'Two more minutes and the plane will be here too. With MRU 3–96 and the lighthouse, you can't go wrong.'

The sound of Roddy's heartbreaking song continued to float up, and was that the sound of Sergeant MacDuff sobbing? Danny prayed

Roddy could keep this singing up, just until the plane went over, just a few more minutes.

Shaking, Danny crouched beside the dodo.

'Ready?' he asked. 'I know you can do this. If you really want to enough. Sometimes we do get what we always dreamed of. I dreamed of an adventure this summer and you showed up! The best adventure ever!'

The dodo clacked his beak softly.

'Follow the plane as far as you can. I'll light your way,' said Danny. 'Don't lose the map. Be safe.'

The dodo reached his giant beak towards Danny. That beak, which he used to be so wary of, now nibbled at his face and hair while the dodo made a soft, cooing sound that Danny had heard once before, to the pigeons; to family.

Danny gulped, then helped the bird hop up on to the top of the balcony.

He ran back to the lantern and gripped its sides. He looked at the sky. The storm had passed. Thin threads of cloud raked across the moon – and then Danny saw it, blinking in the distance, the lights of flight MRU 3–96.

'There!' he shouted. 'There's the plane. Ready, Dodo? It's Operation Homecoming! It's happening. Fly home! Fly! Fly! Fly!'

Danny directed the beam straight on to the bird and held his breath. Silently, the dodo spread his wings, lingered for just a moment and then, without a backwards glance, plunged off.

Danny stood, stunned, for a few seconds, then moved the bright beam this way and that in the dark night sky, searching for the bird.

'Where is he, where is he?' he muttered, his hands shaking.

Then, as the long beam strobed above the island in Clootie Bay, Danny saw something. A blob, awkwardly flapping and bobbing about on the wind.

'That's him! That has to be him! Go! Go! Go!' Danny yelled. 'You can do it, fly home, fly home, Dodo!'

He squinted after the awkward, bouncing shape. Soon, he was barely able to make it out, then, finally, it disappeared beyond the reach of the lighthouse beam and was gone.

Chapter 30

GONE

Danny wasn't sure how long he spent up on the lighthouse balcony in the dark, straining his eyes out to sea, hoping for a final glimpse of the dodo. He barely noticed when Susie came and stood alongside him, scanning the skies too.

Roddy Aye was still singing when Susie put out the lantern and led Danny slowly downstairs. On the grass outside, Sergeant MacDuff was blowing his nose noisily on his handkerchief. Wee Jimmie had pulled his bandages down over his eyes and was lying flat on the grass. Willy McNeish had laid his wheelbarrow down and was sitting propped against it, gazing at nothing in particular. They all seemed to have forgotten about Danny. It was like Roddy had woven a spell over them all with his voice.

Seeing the two children, Roddy finished his song and fell silent. Slowly, everyone woke up. Granny Flora hugged Danny and Roddy Aye winked at him. Wee Jimmie pawed at his bandage, revealing one mad eye and then shook his handcuffed fists at Danny, before being whisked off in an ambulance.

'More dodos, is it?' one of the paramedics asked Wee Jimmie. It was the same two that had picked him up from Granny's farm a few days before. 'Think you need to get back to your hospital bed, friend.'

Sergeant MacDuff began questioning Danny. Why was he up there, what was he doing, didn't he know that it was dangerous in the lighthouse?

'It's my fault!' said Granny Flora, hugging

Danny to her. 'I told him about breaking into the lighthouse when I was a wee lass. It gave him ideas, that's all. He was just after an adventure. No harm done!'

The sergeant frowned.

'Well, it's true, as a young lad I enjoyed an adventure too,' he said. 'Flora, do you remember when me and Archie Campbell caught a weasel and set it free in the Spar one day?'

Granny Flora chuckled.

'Right, well, let's all get home just now,' said the sergeant. 'We can speak again tomorrow, if need be.'

As Granny Flora drove Danny away from the lighthouse he pressed his face to the window, hoping for a final glimpse of the bird. But all he could see was his own reflection, his big blue eyes staring back at him.

Chapter 31

AFTER

When Danny went downstairs the next morning, Susie was already at the kitchen table. Silently, he sat down alongside her.

Granny Flora served Danny a big plate of toast and kissed the top of his head. A single pencil tumbled free of her bun and rattled on to the table.

'No porridge for you today,' she said. 'I owe you a very big apology, Danny. After Wee Jimmie came round here with an air rifle, Sergeant MacDuff got in touch with Glasgow Police and they confirmed that he was a known criminal with a history of thieving and illegally selling things.'

'What things?' said Danny.

'Stolen goods, jewellery, art. Other people's

treasures, basically,' said Granny Flora. 'I trusted him! I thought bad things couldn't happen up here in Kinoussie, but I was wrong. I should have listened to you. Maybe he *had* spotted something in the outbuilding he wanted to steal, and that's why he broke in. That old armchair, perhaps ... Well, we'll likely never know. Glasgow Police took him away this morning for questioning. They'd been wondering where he was hiding out. Now, I must update Moira.'

She disappeared to make more phone calls.

'So, you came to Kinoussie expecting it to be boring,' said Susie. 'But, in fact, you had that adventure you wanted.'

'I went to the island to find treasure,' said Danny. 'And I did. He was a treasure worth more than gold and jewels. I'll never forget him.'

'Me neither,' said Susie. 'He's turned everything I thought I knew about science on its head. I didn't expect that to happen this summer.'

'Where is he now, do you think?' Danny said, staring out of the window. 'I hope he's all right. Please let him be all right.'

'He's probably cruising over France now, clacking his beak with joy!' said Susie.

Danny's face was clouded with worry.

'He'll be OK,' Susie whispered. 'When he took off last night, the wind had dropped, the sky was almost clear. He's on his way home, Danny, just like he wanted. You did it.'

Danny smiled weakly.

'Why don't you put some taramasalata on your toast, to take your mind off things?' Susie suggested.

Danny shook his head. He wasn't hungry. He pushed his plate away. The gentle tick-tack of Roddy's knitting needles drifted over from the corner.

'Thank you for your singing last night, Roddy,' Danny said. 'It saved the do ... Well, it saved the day!'

'Aye!' said Roddy.

'Did you guess what I had in the outbuilding, Roddy?' he asked. 'Did you know who I was trying to help?'

Roddy's eyes sparkled, his knitting needles paused and he smiled at Danny.

'Don't answer that ...' Danny said, and all three of them laughed.

'What will you do today then?' Susie asked. 'Planning another adventure?'

'Nah,' said Danny. 'I think I'll just take it easy.'

'Read some Zac Hanaway comics?'

'Maybe not,' he said. The adventure he'd just had with the dodo was nothing like Zac's adventures in those comics. It was scarier, and harder, and involved more lying. But it was bigger too. It was real. He couldn't explain all that to Susie.

'You can come and help me out in the Spar,' said Susie. 'I'm running the shop today, remember?'

'Could I?' asked Danny.

'Of course!' she said.

'But you have to be in charge,' said Danny, 'of the whole shop.'

Susie leaned in and whispered urgently: 'You've just been in charge of a dodo *and* taught it to fly! Of course you can run the Spar for the day. The only hard thing is helping Willy McNeish remember what he came in for!'

Danny grinned.

'Great,' he said. 'Let's do it.'

The children got up to leave.

'By the way, your mum rang while you were still in bed,' Susie said as they found their coats on the pegs by the front door. 'Granny Flora took the blame for you breaking into the lighthouse, but what will you tell her about everything else? About using the trampoline in the campsite? About attacking Wee Jimmie with buckets and old records?'

Danny thought for a second. Then a second more. A smile crept slowly across his face and he beamed at Susie.

'Easy!' he said. 'I'll just say ... the dodo made me do it!'

BORED OF YOUR BROTHER?

SICK OF YOUR SISTER?

READY FOR A BRAND NEW, SUPERCOOL SIBLING?

READ ON FOR AN EXTRACT FROM THIS
LAUGH-OUT-LOUD ADVENTURE FROM

CHAPTER ONE

CLICK!

CHANGE BROTHERS AND SWITCH SISTERS
TODAY WITH
www.siblingswap.com

The advert popped up in the corner of the screen. Jonny clicked on it instantly. The Sibling Swap website pinged open, showing smiling brothers and happy sisters, all playing and laughing and having a great time together.

What crazy alternative universe was this? Where were the big brothers teasing their little brothers about being rubbish at climbing and slow at everything? Where were the wedgies and ear flicks? What about the name-calling? This looked like a world

Jonny had never experienced, a world in which brothers and sisters actually *liked* each other!

'Oh sweet mangoes of heaven!' Jonny muttered.

It was pretty bonkers, but it was definitely tempting. No, scrap that: it was *essential*. Jonny couldn't believe his luck. Just think what Sibling Swap could offer him.

A new brother. A *better* brother. A brother who didn't put salt in his orange squash, who didn't call him a human sloth, who didn't burp in his ear. That kind of brother.

Jonny had to try it. He could always return the new brother if things didn't work out. It was a no-brainer.

He clicked on the application form.

What could go wrong?

HEAD TO
www.siblingswap.com
TODAY

... your future sibling awaits!

★ ★ ★

Change brothers and switch sisters!

Sometimes you don't get the brother or sister you deserve,
but here at Sibling Swap, we aim to put that right.
With so many brothers and sisters out there,
we can match you to the perfect one!

So what are you waiting for?
Get SWAPPING!

★ ★ ★

- Take the quiz to find your perfect brother or sister
- Meet the founder of Sibling Swap
- Download fun activities and games to play with (or without) your sibling!